EMILY RODDA'S
RAVEN HILL MYSTERIES

CASE #6: DEAD END

Emily Rodda

SCHOLASTIC INC.

New York Toronto London Auckland Sydney
Mexico City New Delhi Hong Kong Buenos Aires

ISBN 0-439-79572-9

Series concept copyright © 1994 by Emily Rodda
Text copyright © 1999 by Scholastic Australia

All rights reserved. Published by Scholastic Inc., 557 Broadway, New York, NY 10012, by arrangement with Scholastic Press, an imprint of Scholastic Australia.

SCHOLASTIC, APPLE PAPERBACKS, and associated logos are trademarks and/or registered trademarks of Scholastic Inc.

12 11 10 9 8 7 6 5 4 3   12 13 14 15 16/0

Printed in the U.S.A.   40
First American edition, September 2006

Contents

1

The writing on
the wall

Help-for-Hire Inc. has caused me a lot of trouble over the years.

I agreed with the idea of setting up a part-time job agency with my friends because I liked the idea of making some extra cash. But I didn't know what I was getting myself into.

Some of our jobs have led us into very weird situations. Sometimes we've found ourselves dealing with crooks as well as clients. We've solved mysteries, helped the cops catch bad guys, and stopped a lot of nasty things from happening. And we've seen a whole lot of action. Dangerous action.

There have been times when I felt like forgetting the whole thing. But in the end I always stayed, and so did everyone else. The six of us stuck together. Liz, Sunny, Richelle, Elmo, Tom . . . and Nick — that's me. One for all and all for one — that sort of thing.

By the time this story I'm going to tell you about happened, I hadn't thought of leaving for a long time. The gang could all be incredibly irritating in their different ways, but I was used to them, and we were a good team. Also, I have to admit, I liked the fact that Help-for-Hire Inc. had developed a big reputation around Raven Hill. We'd been in the paper quite a few times — big city papers as well as the local one, the *Pen* — because of the mysteries we'd solved.

Even my parents had started feeling proud of Help-for-Hire Inc., instead of worrying that it took too much time or that it was dangerous.

Then something happened. Something that changed everything.

○

It started one Friday after school. We had to stay after because we had an appointment to meet this guy — a Mr. Mellborn — who'd called Liz that morning with a job for us — clipping a long hedge, or something. We had to meet him in the school parking lot at four.

Raven Hill High on Friday afternoons is a seething mass of people for five minutes after the final bell, and just about deserted three minutes after that. Practically everyone clears out as fast as they can, to make the weekend seem as long as possible. It's about the only time you see teachers actually running.

We stood back so as not to get crushed in the stampede, then we collected our stuff and wandered down to the parking lot. By the time we got there it was empty except for a dusty brown station wagon with a dent on one side, and a shiny little green hatchback.

The green car belonged to Mrs. Fenelli, one of the crabbiest teachers in the school. The brown heap belonged to the vice-principal, Mr. Harris, who'd been at Raven Hill High for about a hundred years.

"Weak Willy's working late," snickered Tom.

"*Don't* call him that, Tom," snapped Liz.

Mr. Harris's first name was William and the staff called him Bill, at least to his face, but he'd been called Weak Willy by the kids since long before I got to high school. He was a clueless, bony, mumbling sort of guy who had the personality of a soggy tomato sandwich. He couldn't control his classes, his lessons were incredibly boring, he made the same feeble jokes over and over again, and he wore a cheap toupée that was five shades darker than the rest of his hair.

Everyone despised him — except Liz, who felt sorry for him. She's always feeling sorry for hopeless cases.

I couldn't understand why they hadn't fired Weak Willy long ago, let alone why they'd made him vice-principal. But somehow or other he'd gotten the job and then just hung on. About three weeks ago he'd gotten his big chance. The principal went on leave, and Willy took charge.

When I say he "took charge," of course, I'm joking. Willy Harris couldn't take charge of a kid's birthday party, let alone a decent-sized high school. He couldn't handle the principal's job, and he looked more miserable and untidy every day.

"Have you noticed the bags under Weak Willy's eyes lately?" said Tom, as though he'd read my mind. "They're twice as big as they used to be."

So then of course Liz started saying she felt sorry for him again, and the whole argument with Tom started all over again.

I was bored and irritated because we had to hang around. Especially when four o'clock came and went and this Mellborn guy still hadn't turned up. By four twenty-five it seemed to me that we'd been hanging around that parking lot for hours.

The others were getting edgy, too. And they were all showing it in the most *typical* ways.

Liz worried — first because she was going to be late visiting Pearl Plummer, this old woman she shops for on Friday afternoons, and then in case we were waiting in the wrong place.

"I'm sure he said four o'clock in the school parking lot. I'm *positive*," she kept saying. "But maybe he didn't mean Raven Hill High. Maybe he meant another school."

Sunny was being sensible and trying to calm Liz down. "Why would he mean any other school?" she asked calmly. "He knows we all go to Raven Hill High. He's probably stuck in the traffic." While she was talking she was doing push-ups so as not to waste valuable exercise time sitting around. Sunny's like that. Crazy.

Tom was complaining about being hungry. If you'd seen the lunch he had you'd wonder how he could ever eat again, but according to him he was going to faint if he didn't get a snack — half a dozen doughnuts or a couple of hamburgers — to tide him over till dinner.

Richelle was checking out her fingernails, filing off imaginary rough bits, and feeling annoyed. "It's so *rude*," she kept saying. "If you make an appointment, you should at least *try* to be on time."

"That's good, coming from you," Tom jeered in that irritating way he has. "You're *always* late yourself."

"No, I'm not!" hissed Richelle.

4

"Yes, you are."

"No, I'm not!"

And all this time Elmo was pacing around, ruffling his curly hair into even more of a mess than usual. He wasn't complaining, because Elmo hardly ever complains out loud. But everyone knew he was dying to get away so he could go to the *Pen* office.

Zim, Elmo's dad, owns and runs the *Pen*, and Elmo spends every spare minute he has at the office. Lately he'd hardly been out of the place except to go to school, do Help-for-Hire work, and sleep. Zim was incredibly busy because he was about to go away. Some crazy committee voted the *Pen* the best local newspaper in the state, and Zim won a new car and a trip to New Zealand. All I can say is, if the *Pen*'s the best in the state, I'd hate to see the others.

I looked at my watch. It was well after four-thirty. Suddenly I couldn't stand it any longer.

"I'm going home," I said, grabbing my backpack. "This Mellborn character can't expect us to wait for him forever."

"Well, if Nick's going, I am, too," said Richelle.

"Likewise." Tom picked up his own bulging bag.

"Just five more minutes," Liz pleaded.

I shook my head and started walking to the exit gate, with Tom and Richelle following me. But we hadn't gone more than four or five steps when a shrill voice stopped us.

"Nick Kontellis! Tom Moysten! Stop, please! You, too, Richelle! And the rest of you! Come here."

I turned around and saw Mrs. Fenelli beckoning angrily from the school side of the parking lot. Liz, Sunny, and Elmo were already moving toward her, looking nervous. I sighed to myself. What did Fenelli want? If only I'd left ten minutes earlier!

"Come with me, please," Fenelli snapped as soon as we were close enough.

"Um — we're waiting for someone, Mrs. Fenelli," Liz said awkwardly.

"It doesn't look like that to me," said Fenelli. "Come on. Quickly!" She turned around and stalked back up toward the main part of the school. We followed, making faces at one another behind her back, wondering what was going on.

And then we saw it. Huge yellow letters scrawled right across the bricks at the back of the new science building.

DROP DEAD WEAK WILLY

The message hadn't been there when we walked past the science building at the end of school. *Someone's been busy*, I thought.

I heard Tom snickering behind me. The idiot. I spun around and glared at him, and so did Liz and Sunny, but we were too late. Mrs. Fenelli had heard him, too.

"You think it's funny, do you?" she said in a dangerously low voice.

"No," said Tom, smirking.

Her eyes narrowed. "Well, I don't think it's funny, either," she hissed. "And neither will your parents." She stared at the whole group with an icy gaze. "It will be up to Mr. Harris to decide whether the police are called or not. But I hope, I sincerely hope, that they will be."

It dawned on us all at the same moment that she thought we'd painted the graffiti on the wall.

"Hey — no — wait a minute —" Tom spluttered. "You don't think *we* did this, do you?"

"I know you did," Fenelli said grimly.

We just stared at her.

"Mrs. Fenelli, we don't know anything about it," Sunny said after a moment.

Mrs. Fenelli tightened her lips until they were a hard, straight line. She took a breath to reply but, just as she did, who should come around the corner of the building but Mr. Harris himself, on his way to the parking lot.

He wandered over to us, smiling weakly. "What's going on here?" he asked. Then he saw the writing on the wall. His jaw dropped, and slowly a scarlet blush spread over his face from chin to forehead.

"We didn't do it," Tom blurted out, sounding as guilty as sin. I dug my elbow into his ribs. In my experience it's best to just shut up when stuff like this happens.

Weak Willy turned to look first at Tom, then at Mrs. Fenelli.

"Unfortunately, that is untrue," said Mrs. Fenelli firmly. "This boy defaced the wall with yellow spray paint, and these others watched him do it."

We were all so shocked that for a split second none of us could say anything, then we all burst out into loud denials.

Mr. Harris winced and blinked at us as if the noise was hurting his ears. He flapped his hands at us till we quieted down.

7

"Mrs. Fenelli, why do you think these kids are responsible?" he asked nervously. I got the feeling he was a little scared of Mrs. Fenelli.

She drew herself up and threw back her shoulders. "Why?" she spat. "Because I saw them doing it. With my own eyes. I saw them!"

2

Confusion

My first thought was that Mrs. Fenelli had gone crazy. It's surprising that more teachers don't snap, considering what a lot of them have to put up with. If I had to deal with Moysten in class, I'd be worrying about my sanity in five minutes, I can tell you.

"I was about to leave, and I just looked out the window as I closed it," Fenelli was raving on to Weak Willy Harris. She pointed up to the staff room window, which was in another building overlooking the science building. "Imagine how I felt when I saw what these people were doing. I ran down the stairs as fast as I could, but of course by the time I got here they were gone. So I —"

"You must have seen someone else, Mrs. Fenelli," I interrupted as politely as I knew how.

"Are you calling me a liar, Nick Kontellis?" she hissed.

"Well, you're calling *us* liars," Tom piped up. Moysten really is impossible. I stepped hard on his foot and turned to Mr. Harris.

"I'm just saying Mrs. Fenelli made a mistake, sir," I

said smoothly. "She must have seen another group spraying the wall."

He eyed me doubtfully.

"It was you!" screeched Mrs. Fenelli. "I was surprised, I have to say, to see you, Liz, and you, Sunny and Elmo, involved in something like that. Nothing Tom Moysten did would surprise me. But the rest of you people —"

"Where's the spray can, then?" I asked quickly. "It's not here, is it? Whoever did this must have taken the can away. Look, how about we all empty out our bags?"

"There's no point in that," Mrs. Fenelli snapped. "Obviously, since you offer to do it, Nick, you've hidden the can on your way out."

I felt really angry, then. She had an answer to everything.

Liz had tears in her eyes, but she was angry, too. She turned her back on Mrs. Fenelli and looked straight at Weak Willy.

"Mr. Harris, I give you my word of honor that we didn't spray this wall!" she exclaimed.

"That's right," said Sunny flatly, and Elmo nodded.

Weak Willy looked helplessly around. Then finally he turned to Mrs. Fenelli. "Under the circumstances, it might be better just to let the children run along," he said. "If they were responsible, I'm sure they've learned their lesson now."

"Mr. Harris, I *really* think —" Mrs. Fenelli exclaimed in a high voice.

"But we *didn't* —" Liz began, at the same moment.

"That's enough!" Mr. Harris thundered suddenly.

We all jumped. None of us had ever heard Weak Willy shout before. I think he'd surprised himself, too. He licked his lips and took a breath. "I'll give Maintenance a call and have this painted over," he murmured to Mrs. Fenelli. "It was due for a touch-up anyway."

She just glowered at him.

He turned to us. "Off you go now," he said. "We'll say no more about it."

The words were ordinary enough, but Mr. Harris's voice wasn't friendly. His eyes looked hurt. We turned away and left, feeling pretty bad. Obviously despite everything we'd said, Weak Willy still thought that we were guilty.

There was no point going back to the parking lot. Even if Mr. Mellborn had turned up while we were away, he would have left again by now.

"Weak Willy might say no more about it, but Fenelli will, for sure," I muttered as we trudged through the gates.

"She'll spread the story around the faculty lounge as soon as she gets in on Monday," Richelle agreed.

We stopped by the Black Cat Cafe to talk. Liz called Pearl Plummer on my cell phone and told her she'd been held up and would call in tomorrow.

"Brian's going to go insane," Tom muttered gloomily, stirring his hot chocolate.

Brian is Tom's stepfather — *and* a history teacher at the school.

"Well, if he says anything you can just tell him you didn't do it, Tom," said Sunny matter-of-factly.

Tom laughed miserably. "As if he'd believe me," he said. "He'd listen to Fenelli before he'd listen to me any day. He'd listen to *anyone* before he'd listen to me."

Liz glanced at Tom, worried. But I was puzzled about something else.

"Listen," I said. "Let's talk about the main problem. Why did Fenelli lie about seeing us spray that graffiti?"

"She made a mistake," Liz said promptly, putting down her coffee cup. "She saw some other kids there and she ran down and when she saw us in the parking lot she just assumed we were the same kids."

"But she absolutely *insisted* it was us," said Elmo slowly. "And it wouldn't be easy to mix us up with another group. I mean, Richelle's got long, fair hair. Tom's incredibly tall. Nick's very dark. Sunny's Asian-American. I've got curly red hair. Liz is just ordinary, but —"

"Well, thanks very *much!*" exclaimed Liz.

Elmo glanced at her, worried, then realized she was joking. "You know what I mean," he said. "You couldn't really mistake another group for us. The Work Demons, for example, are all guys, and —"

"And all ugly," Tom offered.

"Yes, but the point is, as a group they don't look like us at all. No one looks like us. So how could Fenelli —"

"She's just out to get us," said Richelle. "She must be."

That didn't make sense to me. "Fenelli's sour as a lemon, but why would she want to get us?" I demanded.

Richelle tossed her hair back and looked at me pityingly. "It's because Help-for-Hire's had so much publicity, Nick," she said, as if she was explaining something to a little kid. "She probably thinks we're conceited and it's up to her to take us down a notch."

Sometimes Richelle says things that make you stop and think. And I *did* stop and think about that. But unless Mrs. Fenelli really had gone crazy, I couldn't believe she'd deliberately frame us.

"I think the important thing is how we're going to prove we aren't guilty," said Elmo thoughtfully.

"We *can't* prove it," Tom muttered.

"Yes, we can!" exclaimed Liz. "Mr. Mellborn! He can tell them he made an appointment with us for four o'clock."

"He didn't turn up, Liz," said Sunny flatly. "Do you have his number?"

"No. But he'll be calling me to apologize," Liz said.

"Oh, sure," growled Tom.

And I had to agree with him. Liz has a very unrealistic view of human nature. If Mellborn had decided he didn't want to hire us after all, he'd just forget all about us. He wouldn't call back. And then there'd be no proof that we hadn't stayed after school to write that stupid graffiti on the wall. No proof at all.

3

Bad vibes

When they got home, Liz, Sunny, Elmo, and Richelle told their parents what had happened.

Richelle's father immediately wrote a letter to Mr. Harris complaining that his daughter had been insulted and wrongly accused by Mrs. Fenelli. Liz's mother told Liz to make an appointment to see Mr. Harris on Monday and explain the situation all over again. Sunny's mother laughed at the very thought that Sunny would do such a thing. Elmo's father laughed, too, Elmo said — in between working on a story about Raven Hill waste disposal.

But I knew my parents would worry endlessly about a scandal like that, so I didn't tell them. And Tom didn't tell his mother or Brian, either, though we all told him he should because Brian was bound to find out anyway on Monday morning.

We met up again on Saturday afternoon, to walk seven Great Dane puppies some madman was keeping in a small Raven Hill terrace house until they could be sold. When I say "walk," I'm joking. Those puppies never walked anywhere — they galloped.

They were only ten weeks old, but they were already huge. This made it all the more ridiculous that they were named after the seven dwarfs in the Walt Disney version of *Snow White* — Grumpy, Sleepy, Happy, Dopey, Bashful, Sneezy, and Doc. It was my turn to take Sleepy and Doc, who were less trouble than the others and could be handled as a pair. Everyone else had their hands full with just one.

We talked about the problem all over again while the puppies dragged us around Raven Hill Park. Mr. Mellborn hadn't called Liz back, so even she was starting to wonder if she'd ever hear from him again.

"So we look him up in the phone book," said Sunny, jogging behind Happy, who was practically strangling himself trying to run even faster. "Easy enough. There can't be many people called Mellborn living in Raven Hill."

"He doesn't live in Raven Hill," puffed Liz, trying to stop Dopey from disappearing into a stormwater drain. "He rents out this house with the hedge to someone else."

"We'll have to call every Mellborn in the phone book till we find him, then," panted Tom. He tripped over Sneezy's leash and fell flat on his face. We laughed. Sneezy licked his face sympathetically. "And let's do it before Monday," Tom went on, as if nothing had happened. "I need solid proof for Brian."

The puppies' house was quite near the *Pen*, so after we'd returned them we all went to the office with Elmo.

Because it was Saturday, Zim was the only person in the building. He was sitting in his cluttered little office, working, as usual, and looking frazzled, also as usual.

15

"Can we make a few phone calls, Dad?" Elmo asked, putting his head around the door.

"Oh . . . yes, of course," Zim said, as if he was wondering why we were asking him. "Elmo, I think I should cancel this New Zealand trip. I *can't* leave tomorrow morning! There's so much . . ."

"We'll be fine, Dad," Elmo interrupted. "Really. It's only two issues. Stephen and Mossy and I can handle it. I'll be off from school most of the time, remember."

Zim tugged at his hair, which was as curly and untidy as Elmo's. "I suppose so," he muttered unhappily.

We left him and went on down the narrow hallway into the big back room where the journalists worked. Tom made for the bag of cookies, and Liz grabbed a phone book and started looking up "Mellborn."

"Zim isn't looking forward to his vacation, is he?" Sunny grinned to Elmo. "Does he think the *Pen's* going to fall apart while he's gone?"

Elmo nodded. "Of course. But he hasn't had a break for years, and this trip's such a great opportunity."

Visiting crummy little local newspapers all over New Zealand wouldn't be my idea of a vacation, but Zim and Elmo are obsessed.

"Isn't he scared his new car's going to be stolen while he's gone?" asked Richelle. "You don't have a garage or anything."

I groaned silently to myself. I didn't want Elmo to start on the new car. He'd already bored me to death carrying on about the air-conditioning system and the air bags and antilock brakes. Now he was going to tell Richelle about the specially fitted tracking device that meant it could be located if it was stolen. I'd already heard about that twice.

To avoid having to listen, I took a list of phone numbers from Liz, sat down at one of the journalists' desks, and started calling Mellborns. Eventually, all the others did the same thing. The job didn't take long. And it was useless.

"He must have an unlisted number," groaned Liz, putting down the phone on the last call. "Oh, what are we going to do now?"

"Burn down the school. Have Harris committed to a home for boring losers. Hit Fenelli on the head so she loses her memory, and put her on a slow train to nowhere," joked Tom.

"There's nothing we *can* do," Sunny said, ignoring him. "We'll have to just keep denying we did anything wrong."

"Maybe, when they find out we're in trouble, whoever did it will own up," Liz said hopefully.

I just looked at her. As if.

School was a nightmare on Monday. Mrs. Fenelli had done her work well and by recess it was completely obvious that every teacher had heard the news. All of them — even the ones we liked — looked at us as though we were criminals.

It was typical, really. Most of them probably thought Weak Willy was hopeless. But they didn't like kids saying so. Teachers tend to stick together. They also knew how much the new science building had cost, and they didn't like it being vandalized. But from what one or two of them said to me, it was obvious that the thing they hated most was that we refused to admit we'd done the evil deed.

It didn't matter what we said or did. Fenelli had convinced them all that we were liars. It was pretty hard to take.

Somehow, all the kids had heard about it, too. There was all this whispering and staring going on. Some of them treated us like heroes and followed us around, but since most of them were losers who I wouldn't be seen dead with normally, that wasn't good news.

As soon as I got outside at lunch, Bradley Henshaw and Nutley Frean from the Work Demons came up to me with the rest of their idiot gang behind them. "Heard you've been a naughty boy, Nicky," Bradley giggled at me. He and his brother, Darren, were the founders of the Work Demons.

"You think Zimmer's old man'll put *this* news in the paper?" snickered Nutley Frean. "No way. He only puts in the good stuff about you losers, right?"

"If we'd been caught doing that job, we'd've been slaughtered," said Henshaw. "Help-for-Hire Inc. gets off clean. Call that fair?"

"We–didn't–do–it," I said slowly. "Can you get that into your heads?"

"Oh, right," grinned Frean. "Fenelli was dreaming, was she?"

I couldn't stand this. I turned around and walked away from them. They marched after me, making stupid noises and calling out "Naughty Nicky" in high-pitched voices. The only place I could think of they wouldn't follow me was the library, so I made for that.

When I got inside I found that Tom, Liz, and Richelle were

there, too. Richelle had been crying, and Liz was patting her shoulder. I couldn't cope with any more heavy stuff, so I avoided the girls and sat down next to Tom.

"I've spent the whole morning dodging Brian," he said.

"Well, don't worry, he won't look for you here," I muttered. "It's the last place he'd think to look."

"Yeah. That's what I thought," sighed Tom contentedly. He didn't seem to realize I'd been insulting him. It was tempting to point it out, but I decided to let it pass.

"Have you seen Elmo and Sunny?" I asked instead.

"Sunny's in the gym. No one's going to bother her there, right? No one who values their health. Elmo's over there, reading."

He pointed. Sure enough, there was Elmo slumped in an armchair with his nose in a book.

"Why's everyone making such a big deal about this?" Tom complained. "A little graffiti . . ."

"It's because of what the graffiti said. And because we denied writing it. And because we don't usually do stuff like that," I sighed.

"We didn't do it this time, either," Tom pointed out.

"Apparently that doesn't help. Anyway — the school break will start next week. It'll all have blown over by next term."

"It'd better have," said Tom gloomily.

I didn't want to talk anymore, so I wandered over to the magazine rack and found a fairly new computer magazine. I sat down and pretended to read, but it was hard to concentrate.

I found myself cursing our bad luck. If that Mellborn guy had turned up on time, or if the appointment had been on another day, we wouldn't have been at the school when the graffiti was done. Then none of this would have happened. It had been bad luck from start to finish, right down to Mr. Mellborn having an unlisted number.

All of a sudden, a weird little nervy prickle ran all over me.

Was this just bad luck? Or was it something else? Could someone have planned all this? Someone who was out to get us?

I shook my head and turned another page. Stupid. I was getting paranoid. Why would anyone be out to get us? Except for the Work Demons, we didn't have any enemies.

Did we?

4

Wrong time, wrong place

After school, we went to the Glen, this patch of forest next to Raven Hill Park. Not many people go there except us. There's a clearing there that we use when we want to talk in private.

For the last few months, we'd been going straight from school to the Glen every Monday afternoon — ever since Liz saw this video about business management her father brought home from work. The video was probably nonsense, but Liz got all excited about it. She said a regular weekly meeting was the only way to keep the Help-for-Hire Inc. work organized properly.

It was boring having a formal meeting every week when we saw one another at school all day, but I had to admit it had improved things. And since I'd always been the first to complain when things went wrong, I had to go along with it. Liz's crazes never lasted long, anyway. I knew she'd get sick of it eventually.

I sat against a tree and listened to Liz talk about the work we had lined up for the school break.

"Wednesday and Thursday we're painting the fence at Lawson's Nursery —"

"I can't work on Wednesday," Elmo chipped in. "Wednesday's press night."

"That's okay," Liz said, making a note. "We'll handle it without you. Now. There could be a couple of days' babysitting in the second week. Twins —"

I groaned quietly. I can't stand babysitting.

Liz looked at me severely and went on. "It's a Mrs. Linum on Parker Place. She wants to meet us before she gives us the job. After school tomorrow. Okay?"

Richelle, who'd been checking her hair for split ends, looked up and sniffed. "Can you smell something?" she asked.

"It's only Moysten," I told her. "You should be used to it by now." I ducked as Tom tried to kick me.

"No," said Richelle. "Not that sort of smell. It's like — a campfire or something."

We all sniffed.

"Burning leaves," said Elmo. He looked up and pointed to a billowing black trail that was rising from somewhere behind the trees.

"Smoke! It's coming from the other side of the Glen," Liz said, looking worried. "We'd better go and see what it is."

"It's probably just someone burning leaves in their garden," I yawned. "What are we going to do, report them?"

But Sunny, Liz, Tom, and Elmo were already plunging away down the track that led toward the smoke trail. Elmo was in the lead, excitedly pulling his camera out of its case.

"I suppose he thinks 'Man Burns Pile of Leaves' will make a great headline for the *Pen*," I said to Richelle. "It'd be more interesting than most of the stories they've had lately."

Just then we heard shouting from the direction of the smoke.

"You young hoodlums!" an angry voice roared. "I see you! I know who you are! You! Tom Moysten!"

"Oh, no," I groaned, shaking my head. "What's Moysten done now?"

"Think you're smart? See how you like *this*!" roared the voice savagely.

There was a chorus of loud yells and a high-pitched scream from Liz. I stood, shocked, for a split second, then started running along the track toward the sound, with Richelle close behind me.

"What's happening?" Richelle was gasping as she ran.

We soon found out. Elmo, Liz, Sunny, and Tom came thundering back along the track and nearly knocked us both over. They were covered in black mud and soaked from head to foot.

"Go!" Tom yelled, waving his arms at us. "Get out of here! There's a lunatic with a hose back there!"

Richelle and I turned around and ran back the way we'd come with the others running after us. We ran all the way to the road and when we got there Liz collapsed on the ground, giggling hysterically.

"He soaked us!" she snorted. "He saw us, and he just went crazy!"

"Who? Why?" I demanded. "Liz, stop *laughing*!"

"It was that guy Lennie Frykburg, who lives behind Golden Pines retirement home," panted Tom. "Someone had lit a fire at the edge of the Glen, right next door to him. You know? Where people dump leaves sometimes? There was a pile of leaves. That's what made the smell."

"And all the smoke!" gasped Elmo. "It had blown into his yard and he had clothes on the clothes line, and there were all these little black spots on the sheets, and —"

"But why did he aim the hose at *you*?" Richelle screeched, wrinkling her nose at their wet, black school uniforms.

"He was trying to put out the fire," Sunny said. "And when he saw us, he just started aiming at us as well. We all fell over in the ashes, but he just kept going."

"Has everyone in Raven Hill gone crazy?" I demanded.

No one answered.

❂

As I trudged home a while after that, I was looking forward to a nice, quiet night. I wasn't prepared for trouble. But trouble was waiting for me.

My father met me on the doorstep. He was still in his suit from work. My first thought was panicky. *Why is he home so early? Has something happened to Ma?* But his first words made me realize that it was something else that was wrong. Something to do with me.

"So," he said, "you are home at last, Nicholas."

He turned and went inside, and I followed him. I could tell by the stiffness of his back and neck that he was very upset.

There was no sign of Ma in the kitchen or living room. That was odd at this time of day.

"Your mother is lying down," Dad said, noticing me look around. "She is not feeling well. She called me at work and asked me to come home. She has had a phone call that upset her. Very much."

I sighed impatiently. Fenelli or Weak Willy must have called home to complain about the graffiti after all. I should have known. I should have told Dad when it first happened.

"Dad — it's nothing to worry about," I said.

"Nothing to worry about? Nicholas, I cannot understand how you can say this!" Dad exclaimed, running his hands through his hair. "How could you do such a thing?"

"I didn't do anything, Dad," I muttered. "It's some sort of mistake."

"But this man — this Frykburg — said —"

My stomach lurched. "What?" I burst out wildly. "Mr. *Frykburg?*"

"He called your mother half an hour ago," Dad said. "He told her that you and your friends set fire to a pile of leaves near the park. Nicholas, do you realize how dangerous —"

"Dad!" I broke in desperately. "The guy's a lunatic! He squirted Liz and Tom and Sunny and Elmo with his hose when they went to see where all this smoke was coming from. And I wasn't even with them."

"He says you set the fire, Nicholas," my father said gravely. "You, personally, while the others piled up more leaves to make it burn faster. He says that when you saw him you all ran away, but Liz, Elmo, Tom, and Sunny came back when he was trying to put out the fire."

"Dad — this isn't true!" I said desperately. "You can ask the others."

25

A flicker of doubt crossed my father's face. "This man was very certain, your mother says," he murmured.

"Well, he's completely wrong!" I said. "We had nothing to do with starting that fire, Dad. I promise."

Dad stared at me searchingly for a second, then nodded. "If you say so, Nicholas, I believe you," he said. "There has been a mistake. I will go and tell your mother. She will be very relieved. Then we must tell this man that he is wrong."

He clapped me on the back and went to find my mother. I stood where I was, stunned.

What was going on?

5

No fast fix

Dad called Mr. Frykburg, but couldn't convince him that we hadn't started the fire. His face was dark red when he hung up.

"The man is impossible!" he growled. "He says he saw you clearly."

"He has a grudge against my Nick!" my mother exclaimed angrily. "Why else would he try to blacken his name?"

"It's not just me, Ma," I said. "It's everyone in Help-for-Hire Inc."

Dad looked at me, frowning.

"I can't think of a reason why he'd have a grudge against us," I said. "The job we did for him went fine — it was just clearing out a garage."

The phone rang and Dad answered it. It was Liz for me.

"Have your parents heard from —?" Liz began.

"Yeah," I said, watching my mother and father watching me. "Frykburg called a while ago. Your parents, too, obviously."

"He was *awful*, Nick." Liz's voice was loud, high, and angry, and I moved the phone away from my ear. "He told all these absolute lies to Mom. After I got home and explained, she called him back and he wouldn't even *listen* to her."

"Yeah. Dad called him back, too," I muttered, still keeping an eye on my parents. "Same sort of result."

"He's called everyone's parents! Richelle's *hysterical*, and Tom's in awful trouble, with the school thing and now this. Brian won't believe he's telling the truth — even after Mom spoke to him and told him we all said the same thing. Brian's so awful. He doesn't trust Tom at *all*."

"It has been known for Moysten —" I began. But Liz broke in impatiently.

"I know Tom fibs sometimes. But Nick — we know he isn't lying about this. We were *with* him."

"Not all the time," I said carefully. And quickly moved the receiver even farther away from my ear.

Just in time.

"NICK! WHAT ARE YOU SAYING?!" Liz roared.

She yelled so loudly that even my parents could hear her voice quacking through the receiver. They looked at me, surprised and worried.

Trying to look casual, I turned my back on them and spoke a bit more softly into the phone. "I only mean we went down to the Glen separately," I said, keeping my voice as calm and even as possible. "Tom and Sunny were already there when I arrived. Then Elmo turned up. And you and Richelle didn't come till a few minutes later."

"Well, Mr. Frykburg said we were all together when *you* lit the fire, Nick," Liz said coldly. "So it doesn't matter what we were doing before that, does it?"

"I guess not." She was right, of course.

"Well, all right," said Liz crisply. "Now. Did Mr. Frykburg tell your father he was going to report us to the police in the morning?"

"What?" I was astounded. I glanced again at Dad. "What does he mean, report us —"

My father glared at me and shook his head slightly. I broke off, realizing that he hadn't mentioned this little detail to Ma yet. He didn't want to upset her any more than was necessary.

I cleared my throat. "Liz — maybe we should talk about this in person," I said. "Could we get together after dinner?"

"I suppose we could," Liz said doubtfully. "But I don't know if Tom will be allowed out. And Elmo's busy with Zim. And Mom hasn't even started dinner yet because of all the fuss with Mr. Frykburg. First thing tomorrow would be better. We have to walk the puppies again before school — remember?"

I thought it through quickly and reluctantly decided she was right. "Okay," I said. "See you at seven tomorrow, then."

We said good-bye, and I hung up. I turned to face my parents, shrugged, and made a face.

"This Frykburg guy's called everyone," I said. "I don't know what's going on. None of us do."

I was trying to look cool, but I guess I didn't pull it off, because Ma raced over to me and hugged me.

"Never mind about that awful man, Nick," she soothed, patting my back as though I was seven years old again and someone scary had yelled at me in the street. "Your father will fix him."

I stared over her head to where my father stood, hands in pockets, jingling the change in his pockets and looking thoughtful.

I could tell that he wasn't quite as confident as Ma was that Mr. Frykburg could be "fixed" so easily.

Neither was I.

○

The next morning everyone was on time for once, even Richelle. We couldn't wait to talk. We collected the puppies and made for the park as fast as we could go.

"Dad says if the police turn up at school I have to call him right away," Richelle gabbled as we ran down the sidewalk. "Oh, this is so *embarrassing!*"

"It's more than just embarrassing," muttered Tom. "It's a disaster as far as I'm concerned."

"Mom's really upset," Liz said. "Dad's worried about Frykburg spreading stories about us. And Pete keeps asking if I'm going to go to jail. I mean, I know he's only little, but —"

"*Jail!*" shrieked Richelle.

"Don't forget, the police know us. And anyway, you don't get put in jail for a first offense like that," said Elmo.

"It's our second offense," Tom pointed out gloomily. "There was the graffiti on the wall of the science building, remember."

Sunny shook her head. "Listen," she said firmly. "This is crazy. You're all talking as though we've actually *done* something. But we haven't. We're completely innocent."

"But we can't prove it," I said grimly. "And that's what I want to talk about."

We'd reached the park by now. Thankfully, the puppies

slowed down as soon as their feet hit the dewy grass. They started sniffing around, and we were able to walk instead of run.

The others were all staring at me. I took a deep breath. I wanted to get this right without seeming too crazy.

"It just seems too big a coincidence that twice in two days we've been accused of doing something wrong, and both times it's been impossible to prove we were somewhere else at the time," I said.

Elmo stopped completely and Sneezy, who'd been on the trail of some particularly delicious smell, yelped in protest.

"You're saying maybe we're being *framed?*" he asked, running his hand through his tangled hair.

Richelle looked at me, her eyes wide, and nodded slowly.

But Sunny snorted. "That's ridiculous! That would mean that Mrs. Fenelli and Mr. Frykburg were in some sort of conspiracy with each other to get us."

I had to defend myself, though I knew I was on shaky ground. "They could know each other," I said. "They could each have some reason we don't know about to —"

"What reason?" snapped Liz, patting Sleepy and Doc in turn. "We haven't done anything to either of them."

"Fenelli's always hated me," Tom put in helpfully.

"Mrs. Fenelli hates everyone," said Richelle. "Including Mr. Harris, I suppose. She probably thinks she should be principal instead of him. She's been at the school even longer than he has. So the whole thing fits, doesn't it?"

I stared at her, trying to follow her reasoning, then gave up. "What do you mean, Richelle?" I asked slowly.

She blinked at me. "Well, you were the one who said we were being framed, Nick."

"Yes, but what's Mrs. Fenelli hating Mr. Harris got to do with it?"

Richelle sighed. "Well, if she *liked* him, Nick," she said very patiently, "she wouldn't have written drop dead weak willy, would she? She would have written something else."

Now it was my turn to stop dead. "You think *Fenelli* sprayed the wall?"

Richelle tossed back her long fair hair. "Of course she did," she said. "Just like that horrible Frykburg man set fire to the Glen."

"Richelle —" Liz began.

But Richelle was going on. "I mean, that's the only thing that makes sense. Mrs. Fenelli and Mr. Frykburg swore they'd seen *us* spray the wall and light the fire. And we didn't, did we? But the wall *was* sprayed, and the fire *was* lit. So — they must have done it themselves."

Elmo was gazing at her in awe. "She's right, you know," he muttered, as if he couldn't believe it.

Richelle tossed her head again. "Well, I don't see why you're so surprised," she said crossly. "I *can* work things out when I want to, you know."

She glared at Elmo for a moment, then smoothed her hair carefully. "Anyway, that's settled," she sighed. "When the police come we'll just tell them that everything was Mrs. Fenelli's and Mr. Frykburg's fault. And that will be that."

I heard Liz give a little groan, and raised one eyebrow at her.

I knew she was thinking just what I was thinking: *If only it were that simple . . .*

"Defending ourselves that way isn't going to be too easy," said Elmo, putting our thoughts into words.

Sunny shook her head. "We're not going to defend ourselves," she said calmly.

Amazed, we all looked at her.

"If we get hauled away by the police, then babble out some story about a conspiracy, we'll look guilty," Sunny said. "So we're not going to do that. We're going on the attack. We won't wait for the police to come to us. We'll go to them."

6

Police in the picture

Tom and Richelle didn't want to go to the police, but Liz, Elmo, and I agreed with Sunny. After all, a lot of the Raven Hill police knew us because of the crimes we'd helped solve. Our story might seem weird, but we'd been involved in weird things before and we'd never lied to them.

We dropped the puppies back at their house, then walked up to Raven Hill Road and on to the police station.

"We'll be late for school," Richelle moaned, as we went through the doors.

"What, you're scared you'll get into trouble?" I jeered at her. "What trouble could be worse than the mess we're in now?"

If only I'd known what was to come, I wouldn't have said that.

The officer at the front desk wasn't one we knew, unfortunately.

"What can we do for you?" she asked.

"We need to speak to someone about a problem we have," said Liz.

"What sort of problem?" asked the officer.

It was a natural question, but Liz hesitated. I could see that she wasn't quite sure how to go on.

Just at that moment, another police officer came out of one of the back offices. She had her head down and was frowning, as though she was thinking hard about something. Then she looked up, and to my relief, I recognized her. It was Greta Vortek, who we'd worked with one time when we were investigating some strange events at the Raven Hill Library.

"Officer Vortek!" I called out. "Greta!"

Greta Vortek looked over to me. A weird expression crossed her face. The welcoming grin I'd expected didn't appear.

Uh-oh, I thought. I was pretty sure I knew what that meant.

The officer at the desk turned to look at Greta, too. "You know these kids?" she asked. "They want to talk to someone about —"

"I'll handle it," Greta said. She beckoned to us. "Come on in," she said. This time she smiled, but the smile was a worried one and disappeared quite quickly.

We followed her into a little office in the back room, collecting chairs to sit on on the way.

"Do your parents know you're here?" she asked, as she sat down behind the desk.

We shook our heads. "We just decided to come in," Liz said awkwardly. "We need to talk to you."

"Yes, you do, unfortunately," Greta sighed. She glanced at her notebook, then seemed to come to a decision, and went on. "This morning I took a call from a Mr. Frykburg about you," she said slowly. "What he said surprised me."

"What he says isn't true!" Richelle burst out. "He started that fire himself, and for some reason he blamed us."

Greta glanced at her, frowned slightly, and tapped her pen on her notebook again. "You people — well, you've never been in trouble before, have you? Quite the opposite," she said.

"That's why —" I began, but she cut me off.

"Mr. Frykburg seems to think that maybe you've started to get a bit . . . well . . . conceited, you know? 'Too big for their britches' is the way he put it."

"That's not true," Liz exclaimed. "You know that, Greta. You know us."

"I thought I did," Greta Vortek said reluctantly. "And I was so sure Mr. Frykburg had the wrong idea that I called your principal to confirm that your behavior at school had been as usual."

She paused. I made myself go on looking at her and not glance at the others. *Stay cool*, I told myself. But my stomach had turned over. Obviously, Weak Willy had given Greta an earful.

"Mr. Harris told me that there had been a problem with graffiti last week," Greta went on. We all tried to talk, but she held up her hand.

"Let me finish. He downplayed the whole thing. He was very tolerant, I thought. He said that — well, that things have been a bit quiet for Help-for-Hire lately, and that in his opinion you're missing being in the spotlight. So you decided to — stir things up a bit."

"That's complete —" I began angrily.

Greta held up her hand again, to stop me. "The thing that worries me is this," she said. "He said that you claimed you had nothing to do with the graffiti, even though one of the teachers said she'd actually seen you doing the damage."

"She was wrong," said Sunny flatly.

Greta's brow wrinkled. "I could cope with one case of mistaken identity, Sunny," she said slowly. "But I'm having trouble with two. I'm sure you can understand that."

Richelle leaned forward. "Greta, don't you understand? We're being framed," she said earnestly.

Here, in the cold light of the police station, it sounded ridiculous, even to me. And one look at Greta's face made it absolutely clear that there was no way she was going to buy it. No matter what we said. No way.

We spent another half hour with Greta, but the situation didn't improve. Finally, she sent us off to school, saying she'd make arrangements to interview us all separately, with our parents present.

"That's so it can be official," muttered Tom, as we left. "Our parents are supposed to protect us. It's kind of a joke, in my case."

No one said anything about us being late for school. I think Greta must have called Weak Willy to tell him we were with her.

Everyone seemed to have heard about the fire somehow, and no matter what we said, a lot of them obviously didn't believe us when we said we hadn't lit it. Like Greta Vortek, they might have been able to swallow that we'd been wrongly accused once. But twice? No.

As for the idea that Frykburg had started the fire himself — Why would he? everyone asked. The Glen's right next door to his house. If the fire had gotten out of hand, more than his laundry would have been ruined. His whole house might have burned down.

It was easier to believe the other alternative: that we'd gotten bored and started making trouble for fun. That we thought we could get away with it because we had a special relationship with the cops.

It was a miserable morning. At lunchtime Liz and Richelle tried to get in to see Mrs. Fenelli, but she wouldn't see them. I tried Weak Willy, but his secretary said he'd gone home because he wasn't feeling well.

He thinks he's *not feeling well*, I thought, trudging off to the library to join the others, dodging Nutley Frean and Bradley Henshaw on the way. *He should have my problems. Then he'd know what feeling sick is all about.*

7

Parker Place

After school we met at the gate and walked to Parker Place to see Mrs. Linum about the babysitting job.

Parker Place is on my route when I'm delivering the *Pen* on Thursday mornings. It's a little dead-end street tucked away behind an old empty factory right at the edge of Raven Hill. I'd always thought it was such a depressing place.

When we finally got there, we slowly walked along looking at the house numbers, counting down to number 24 where Liz said the Linums lived. I'd never noticed number 24 when I'd been delivering the *Pen*. A lot of the houses in the street didn't have numbers at all and, anyway, I always just raced down and back as fast as I could.

The Parker Place houses are all really small and plain. They line one side of the street, facing the factory, which takes up the whole of the other side.

"Nice view," Tom said sarcastically.

Sunny frowned. "These houses are tiny. Imagine looking after twins in one of them."

"We won't have to imagine it soon. We'll be *doing* it," I said gloomily.

The street looked even worse than it did when I saw it on my paper route in the early morning. Even though it was the afternoon, it was dim and the houses were shut up tight. All of them had bars on the windows. Some of them even had their curtains drawn. The factory loomed above us, cutting out sound as well as light. It was awfully quiet, except for a few police sirens howling in the distance.

A real estate agent, like Liz's father, would probably call it a peaceful spot. Code for depressing hole.

Richelle wrinkled her nose.

"Wouldn't you hate to live here?" she whispered. "It's so depressing. And it smells."

"It's just damp. The factory blocks all the sun," Elmo said.

We reached the last house in the street and stopped. Liz shook her head in frustration and pointed at the house number. "Number twenty-two!" she said crossly. "So where's twenty-four?"

"Well, obviously there is no twenty-four," I said dryly.

"You must have written down the number wrong, Liz," exclaimed Richelle. "Oh, how *annoying*!"

"I didn't write it down wrong! And you can take the job messages yourself, Richelle, if you think you can do better than me!" snapped Liz. She isn't usually crabby, but as I said, we'd had a hard day.

"Maybe it was twenty," Tom suggested. "Mrs. Linum might have said, 'Number twenty, *door* pale green,' or something like that, and you *thought* she said —"

Liz went pink. "It wasn't twenty!" she insisted. "Mrs. Linum didn't say anything about her door! She said twenty-four!"

"It doesn't matter, anyway," said Sunny calmly. "We'll just ask at one of the other houses." She looked around. "It's such a little street — someone's sure to know where the Linums live."

But Liz was absolutely determined to prove she wasn't wrong. There was a patch of overgrown grass and a few bushes at the end of the street, between number 22 and the factory on the other side. Someone's idea of a park, I suppose, but the only sign of life was an overflowing Dumpster.

"Maybe number twenty-four is behind here," Liz said. She plunged into the long grass and started wading through it.

"Come back, Liz!" screeched Richelle. "There might be snakes. Or rats!"

Liz didn't turn back. She can be so irritating when she wants to. The wailing of sirens was much louder now. The sound of it was nearly driving me crazy.

"Liz!" I yelled. "There's nothing there."

But Liz had stopped at the Dumpster and was pulling something out. She waved it at us.

"Look! A handbag!" she called. She started struggling back through the grass toward us. "A perfectly good handbag."

She was opening the handbag as she walked.

"Hey!" she exclaimed as she reached the edge of the grass. "It's full of stuff."

"Let's see!" Tom galloped over to look, and the rest of us trailed after him.

"Look at that!" Liz said excitedly, looking through the bag.

"There's a wallet and a watch and some rings and a really nice handkerchief and some credit cards —"

And that was when, suddenly, I got this really bad feeling.

"Liz!" I said, practically choking on the word. "Drop that thing!"

She stared at me, puzzled. "But someone's lost this, Nick. They'll want it back."

And just at that moment the sound of the sirens came up the street in a wave of sound. We whirled around to see an ambulance and two police cars swooping down the street toward us.

We just stood there, paralyzed, as the ambulance screeched to a stop right in front of us. Two guys in white coats jumped out, threw open the back doors, heaved out a stretcher and shot through the gate of number 22. They didn't even look at us.

They didn't have to. They were leaving us to the cops. The cops were out of the police cars and swarming all over us in two seconds, asking our names, checking us out for knives — the whole bit.

And they were taking the handbag from Liz, and looking at us as though we were something they'd just found under a rock.

"How did you come by this?" one of them said.

"I . . . found it," Liz stammered. She looked all confused. She didn't know what was going on.

But I did. I knew exactly.

And so did all the rest of them when the ambulance guys came back out of number 22 carrying an old woman on a stretcher. The old woman was very pale. She had an oxygen mask over her face, her eyes were closed, and she had a huge red bruise on her forehead. A frizzy-haired younger woman was stumbling along beside the stretcher, holding the old woman by the hand.

When she saw us she pointed and clutched the hand of the policewoman who was walking beside her. Greta Vortek.

"That's them!" she screamed.

There was a second's stunned silence. Greta looked at us, her face hard, baffled, and grim.

"We haven't done anything!" shrilled Richelle, her blue eyes wide with panic. She grabbed my arm and burst into tears.

Greta's hard expression wavered. She murmured something to the frizzy-haired woman. A question.

The woman's face twisted with anger. "Of course I'm sure," she hissed. "I saw them, didn't I? I heard them laughing. I looked out and I saw them in Josie's backyard, clear as day. They had her purse. They ran off around the side. I went in and found her — like this."

8

Big trouble

After that, it was just a blur. Like a terrible, confused nightmare.
I kept thinking: *This can't be happening.*

I remember this huge, red-headed cop who was holding my
arm. His mouth twisted and he turned away and muttered,
"What kind of kids are you?"

It was like I could hear my own voice from a long way away
as I said, "We didn't do this. We didn't go near that old lady.
We found the handbag in the Dumpster."

But it was as though he was deaf. His eyes didn't even blink.
But his grip tightened on my arm as he led me toward the police
cars, just in case I tried to run.

I was put in a car with Tom and Elmo. They were both so
pale and scared-looking, sitting there in the backseat, that I
hardly recognized their faces as I got in. I suppose I didn't look
much better.

Two police climbed into the front, and we were driven to
the police station. Liz, Sunny, and Richelle went in the other
police car, I suppose. Anyway, they were at the station when we
got there.

They got numbers from us and called our parents. Zim was away in New Zealand by then, so Elmo told them to call Miss Moss at the *Pen* office. He's got an aunt, but I don't think he thought about her. When he thinks of home and family, he thinks of the *Pen*. I gave them Dad's number at work. It was hard to imagine him taking the call, but it was even harder imagining what my mother might do if the police called her at home.

It was so weird to be in the police station like this. We'd been there plenty of times before, but then we'd been giving statements — helping the police. This time we were on the other side.

We sat, waiting, hardly knowing what to say to one another. It wasn't easy to think, either, but I tried.

That old lady's neighbor claimed she'd seen us running away with the old lady's handbag. We'd been found outside the house. We had the handbag with us. As far as the police were concerned, we were guilty.

But we weren't. I knew it was important to keep remembering that.

"We've been set up. But all we have to do is tell the truth," I said aloud. "The whole truth, and nothing but the truth. Agreed?"

"Of course," said Sunny. "What else?"

Tom wet his lips. "The truth won't help," he muttered.

"Of course it will, Tom!" Liz exclaimed.

He smiled slightly. When Moysten smiles it's usually a clown's grin. But not this time. This time it was just a bitter twist of the lips in his dead pale face.

"We told the truth about the graffiti. We told the truth about the fire. Did that help?" he asked.

"This is different, Tom," Richelle said.

"Is it?" he asked, still with that awful little smile twitching at the corner of his mouth.

Richelle sighed. "Of course it is," she said scornfully, checking out her face in the mirror she carries around with her. "Now they'll *have* to believe we're being framed. As if we'd bash up an old lady!"

She seemed to think that settled the matter.

I don't know if she was surprised, later, to find herself charged with assault and theft. I certainly wasn't. And I don't think any of the others were, either.

We all told the truth. And maybe our parents and Miss Moss believed us — or pretended to. But no one else did.

That was because no one doubted the word of the frizzy-haired neighbor who said she'd seen us running out of the old woman's backyard with her handbag.

The neighbor's name was Eleanor Meisner. She'd lived in Raven Hill all her life. She'd worked night duty at Raven Hill hospital for twenty years. She'd described us to the cops on the phone when she called for help. She'd pointed us out when she saw us again.

And our story about going to Parker Place about a job didn't hold water. Mrs. Linum and her twins didn't exist — on Parker Place or anywhere else in Raven Hill that the police could discover. We couldn't prove that anyone had called us about a job at all. The whole thing sounded like something we'd made up.

They told us it would be easier for us if we admitted we were guilty. But of course there was no way we were going to do that, so eventually they gave up. They filled out some forms saying what we were charged with, and told us the date that we had to be in court. It was three weeks away.

I remember thinking, *This is going to be the longest three weeks of my life.*

Then we were released on bail. Miss Moss put up the money for Elmo. Dad, Richelle's father, and Liz's mother offered to help, but she wouldn't hear of it.

"I'll get it back," she said, quite cheerfully. "Elmo's not going to run away. We've got a paper to get out. Right, Elmo?"

Elmo's freckles looked like dark spots all over his face because the skin underneath was so white. But he still managed a smile.

I don't know how he did it. I couldn't have smiled if I tried.

That night, I was still awake at two A.M., trying to will myself to sleep. It wasn't just that I was tired. I wanted sleep to blot out my thoughts. I wanted to forget everything — especially the scene when Dad and I finally got home.

Mom was sitting there in the living room in the dark. I think she'd been crying for hours. When we came in and Dad turned on the light, she jumped up, threw her arms around me, and went on crying.

"Nick, Nick, you will go to jail. You will be marked for life as a criminal, Nick," she sobbed. She was shaking all over and clinging to me. It was awful.

And then my father did something I'll never forget. He put his arms around both of us and he said, "We are a family. Whatever comes of this, we will still be a family."

Normally, I'd have been completely embarrassed. And it *was* a bit embarrassing, I have to admit. But it was comforting as well, and it made Mom stop crying.

I appreciated what Dad had said even more later, when he came in to see me in my room after Mom had gone to bed.

He told me he'd be contacting his lawyer in the morning and taking me to see him.

"And when we see Mr. Lucius, Nicholas, you are to tell him exactly, but exactly, what *really* happened. Yes?"

It was then I realized that he thought I was guilty.

"Dad, I didn't do it," I muttered.

He looked at me steadily. "I am not saying you began this thing knowing where it would lead," he said. "But your friends — I cannot forget that you may have been . . . influenced by them to do something foolish. And that things may have gotten out of hand. Young Elmo — he has no mother. He is quiet, but who knows what is going on in his mind? Tom is an amusing boy, and your mother is fond of him, but always he is in trouble at school and with his stepfather. Sunny, like Tom, is from a broken home. She is independent and adventurous — always wanting action. You say it yourself."

I shook my head desperately. "What about Liz? Richelle? Surely you don't think —"

"I do not say that Liz would willingly hurt another person," my father said gravely. "But I do say that Liz would do anything to protect her friends. And Richelle will always believe what she wants to believe. So."

It was strange, but I wasn't angry. I didn't blame him for thinking I was guilty. I probably would have thought I was guilty, too, if I'd been in his place. So it wasn't hard to speak quite calmly.

"Dad, everything you've said is true — sort of," I told him. "But Help-for-Hire Inc. hasn't done anything wrong. Like I told them at the station — someone's set us up. I don't know who, and I don't know why. But I'm going to find out."

He looked at me for a long minute, then he patted my shoulder and left me alone.

What I'd said sounded like a kid's boast or something out of a movie. But I meant it, every word of it. I knew that the only way we were going to save ourselves was to find out who was out to get us.

And get them first.

9

Runaway

I didn't go to school the next day. In the middle of the morning, Dad and I went to see Mr. Lucius, Dad and Mom's lawyer in the city. Dad made me wear my suit.

Mr. Lucius was a very tan, very thin guy who wore rimless glasses and smiled with his lips closed. I thought he looked more like a gangster boss than a lawyer, but Dad seemed to trust him. I told him the whole story, and he wrote everything down. I don't think he believed a word of it.

When we got home, Mom had this big meal ready — lunch meat on a platter and all kinds of different salads. I wasn't hungry, but I sat down and ate as much as I could. So did Dad. We both knew she'd made all this stuff because she was desperate to do something to help.

After that, Dad went to work. "I rely on you to stay here with your mother for the rest of the day, Nicholas," he said as he said goodbye to me. "She will not want to be alone."

Well, yeah. But what he was *really* saying was: "Don't go out and get into trouble."

I nodded and promised and went back inside. I helped Mom

clean up the lunch things. Then she insisted I go and have a rest. She said that sleep would make me feel better. She said I looked awful.

"You don't look too good, either, Ma," I said, trying to grin, but she took me quite seriously and nodded.

"I will rest also," she said. "We must both keep up our strength, for your father's sake."

I went to my room, stripped off my clothes and tie, and lay down, just to please her. I was positive that I wouldn't sleep. Unlike Moysten, who'd probably spend all day in bed if he didn't have to get up to eat, I don't like sleeping in the daytime. But I must have been even more tired than I thought, because all I remember is turning over and pulling up my quilt. Then, nothing.

When I woke up, I could tell by the dimness of the light at my window that it was very late in the afternoon. I rolled over and looked at my bedside clock. Four-thirty! I couldn't believe I'd slept so long.

The phone was ringing. I could hear the sound dimly through all the doors Mom had closed to keep my room quiet. Maybe that was what had woken me. I lay, blinking, for a moment, then I slowly got up and sat on the edge of the bed. *Ma was right,* I thought. *I do feel better now. Much better.*

It was easier to think, I felt less shaky, and things didn't seem quite as nightmarish as they had before. And strangely enough, I was hungry again.

I pulled on some clothes and left my room, heading for the

kitchen to find some food. As I walked closer, I could hear my mother talking on the phone. "No, no!" she was saying. "Nicholas has been here, with me, all afternoon. And this morning with his father."

What now? I thought. I jogged the rest of the way to the kitchen.

Ma was standing in her apron with pastry all over her hands, holding the phone between her shoulder and her chin. "Yes, yes, I am sure he will," she was saying. She glanced up as I came in, and half turned her back, as if to keep me out of the conversation.

"Oh, yes . . . of course I will," I heard her say. "He is a naughty boy, to worry you like this . . . Yes. Good-bye."

She carefully hung up, using two fingers, and smiled at me brightly. She didn't know how much I'd heard. I think she was trying to decide if she could get away with pretending the call had nothing to do with me.

No way.

"What is it?" I asked, as she went back to the pastry she was making. "Ma? Who was that? Why were they asking about me?"

She knew I wouldn't let her off the hook. Besides, she wanted to talk about it, and I was the only one around.

"Tom's mother is worrying because he has not yet come home from school," she said, kneading away at the pastry dough in its bowl. "She thought he might have come here."

Just then the phone rang again. I picked up the receiver quickly.

"Nick?"

It was Liz. I was really glad to hear her voice.

"Nick, is Tom with you?" she asked.

"No," I said, a bit annoyed. "His mother just called. I don't know why everyone's panicking about Moysten. It's not very late. He's probably at Sunny's. Or even at the *Pen*, with Elmo."

"He's not!" Liz exclaimed. "I've called the *Pen*. And Sunny's just turned up here. She's with me now. She was at school today. She saw Tom there. Nick, do you know what she says?"

"What?"

"She saw Tom before school started. They were the only ones of us who were there. Elmo and Richelle stayed away, too. Tom was complaining because Brian had made him go. She said he was really angry, and Nutley Frean was hanging around him and everything and —"

"Yes?"

"Well, Sunny was really worried about him, but then the bell rang. You know on Wednesdays Tom has two art classes before recess? And he and Sunny have different English and math classes after that? Sunny thought she'd have a chance to catch up with him at lunch. But hold on a sec —"

She broke off and there was a clatter as she put down the receiver. Then I could hear her talking to someone. It sounded like her little brother.

"Liz? Liz!" I shouted. "Sunny? Someone pick up the phone!" I saw Ma biting her lips as she plunked the lump of pastry onto a board and started rolling it out. I could tell that she was really curious about what was happening, but was trying not to show it.

Liz finally picked the phone up again. "Sorry. Pete came in and I didn't want him to hear me," she said. "It's all right. He's gone again now. The thing is, Nick, at lunchtime, Sunny couldn't find Tom anywhere. She looked and looked. But he was nowhere. And he didn't turn up at any of the afternoon classes."

I made a disgusted sound. "Moysten strikes again," I said. "He'll just make it worse for himself, ducking out of school. Brian'll be furious."

"Yes," said Liz. But she said it sort of vaguely. As if there was something else on her mind. I could hear Sunny murmuring something in the background. A faint warning bell sounded in my head.

"Liz," I said, turning away from Mom's curious, worried eyes. "What is it? What's the real problem?"

"It's just . . . just that Sunny went home before she came here," Liz said slowly. "And her sister, Sarah, was there."

"So?" I thought I was going to go crazy with impatience.

"I'm telling you. Well, Sarah told Sunny that this afternoon — at about two o'clock — she was coming back into Raven Hill on the bus and she saw Tom. He was standing on the opposite side of the road, hitching a ride."

"What?!"

"Sarah said she only saw him for a few seconds. It might not have been Tom, but she's pretty sure it was. He was wearing his school uniform, without the tie, and he had his backpack with him. He was eating something out of a paper bag. And while Sarah was actually watching, a white van stopped and he got in! And no one's seen him since. Nick . . . Sunny and I think he's run away."

My stomach went into a knot. I felt my face get hot. I don't think I've ever been so angry. My mind was bubbling and

54

whirling around like water boiling in a saucepan, but one thought kept bobbing up to the surface.

We were due in court in three weeks. We were going to claim that we were completely innocent. And now Moysten — the stupid, irresponsible idiot! — had made himself look completely guilty by running away.

How did that make the rest of us look?

Not good. Not good at all.

10

The big question

The only hope we had was that Sarah had made a mistake and the guy she'd seen hitching out of town hadn't been Tom at all. After all, as Liz said hopefully, Sarah had only seen him through a bus window.

But as evening became night, and Tom still hadn't turned up, that hope faded.

I should have known. That description Sarah had given sounded so likely. Eating something out of a paper bag. That would be Moysten. Even running away he'd never forget his stomach.

I'd gotten Dad to agree to me doing the usual Thursday morning *Pen* delivery with the others. He wasn't too happy about it, but he knew that there was no other way the paper could get out.

It was very early, and still dark and cold, when we met up at the back of the *Pen* building and started loading papers onto the wagons. Elmo looked pale as a ghost and had dark circles under his eyes. He'd been up very late while the paper went to press.

Now he was fussing around, asking if we thought the issue looked good and what we thought of the headline and so on. He didn't get much response out of anyone. Richelle just wanted to complain about how tired she was. Liz, Sunny, and I were talking about Tom.

"I can't believe he'd be so stupid as to get in a strange car," Liz worried. "His mother's frantic."

Richelle straightened up from her wagon, stretched her back, and shrugged.

"Richelle, aren't you worried?" exclaimed Liz angrily. "Don't you *care* that no one knows where Tom is?"

Richelle yawned delicately and shook her hair back. "There's no need to worry. For sure he's gone to his dad's place at the shore," she said.

"Well, he hasn't turned up there yet, Richelle," Sunny muttered. "His mother called his father last night. And this morning."

Richelle looked at her pityingly. "Tom's father wouldn't admit Tom was there," she said. "He's completely irresponsible. He'd hide Tom from the police without even thinking about it, if Tom asked him to." She put her head on one side. "You should wear green more often, Sunny," she added, looking approvingly at Sunny's track pants and top. "It looks good on you."

She went back to loading her wagon. Sunny pressed her lips together and started doing the same thing, very fast. Liz looked at them both helplessly. But Elmo and I exchanged glances and he nodded slightly. He thought what I did. That Richelle was perfectly right. Not about Sunny wearing green, but about Tom's father. He *would* lie to protect Tom. And even if the police paid him a visit, there were hundreds of places in that area where Tom could hide.

Sunny had reorganized our routes so that we could cover Tom's usual territory between the five of us. It was going to make the delivery run a bit longer, but at least I didn't have to go to Parker Place. Miss Moss's assistant was going to take some papers there in her car, later on.

"Mossy thought it'd be a bad idea for any of us to be seen around there, Nick," Elmo explained. "If anyone saw you it might — you know — give them the wrong idea."

"You mean they might think I was back to hit another old lady on the head," I muttered.

"Something like that," he said calmly.

Great.

"We need to talk," I said abruptly. "Talk for real, I mean. We've got to do something about this situation."

"We can't stop to do that now!" objected Elmo, who was already in a fever of impatience. "We've got to get the *Pen* delivered."

I started to say something like, "What does that matter?" but Liz cut me off quickly. She didn't want an argument.

"We'll go to the Black Cat for breakfast as usual. When we've finished," she said firmly. "We can talk then."

At the Black Cat Cafe, much later, we all sat around eating and drinking like we often did on Thursday mornings after the *Pen*

delivery. Before coming we'd collected our pay from the office and used the phone there to call Tom's house to see if there was any news. There wasn't, except that his mom had called the police. She'd been hoping to avoid that but, as she said, she couldn't wait any longer. Tom's father was still insisting Tom wasn't with him.

It was much quieter at our table without Tom munching, slurping, making weak jokes, and chattering like a parrot. There was more room without his bony elbows and gesturing hands taking up all the space. And for once nothing got spilled, because Tom wasn't there to spill it.

It was a lot more comfortable. But it was miserable.

"I never thought I'd say this," I said, after a while. "But I miss him."

"Last night you told me you hoped you'd never see his stupid face again," Liz said, looking down at the croissant crumbled on her plate.

"Yeah, well, you do realize he's messed up things for us, as well as himself, by running," I said.

"Oh, that's ridiculous!" Richelle snapped. "It won't affect us at all. Everyone knows Tom ran away only because he doesn't get along with Brian, and Brian made him go to school and everything."

"*We* know that, Richelle," Liz said gently. "But the police don't."

Elmo stirred his hot chocolate, lifted it to his mouth, then put it down again as though suddenly he didn't want it. "When they released us we all promised we'd stay in Raven Hill till the court hearing," he said. "Tom's broken the conditions of his bail. That's really serious."

Sunny moved restlessly. "Well, we can't just sit here talking about it," she said. "We've got to *do* something."

"What are we supposed to do?" Richelle demanded. "I mean, there's nothing we *can* do, is there?"

It was time for me to say what I'd come here to say.

I leaned forward. "There is. We can try to work out who's trying to frame us. Why Fenelli lied about seeing us write the graffiti, and Lennie Frykburg lied about seeing us light the fire, and that woman — Eleanor Meisner — lied about seeing us run out of the old woman's house in Parker Place. None of them had any reason to want to hurt us. We don't even know the Meisner woman. So someone must have *made* them lie. By blackmail or threats or some other way. We've got to find out who that someone is."

Elmo looked up, his eyes bright. And even Liz looked hopeful. But Richelle just went on drinking her fruit juice, as though she hadn't been listening, and Sunny shook her head.

"You're dreaming, Nick," she said flatly.

"Why?" I demanded. "We've solved lots of cases before. And we've got much more reason than we usually have to do it this time."

Liz nodded vigorously. "And it's the best way to get Tom back, Sunny," she said. "If we find out who's responsible for all these crimes, there'll be no reason for him to stay away anymore, will there?"

Sunny picked up her bag and stood up. "I'm going to the gym," she said flatly. "I'll talk to you later, Liz."

We sat there watching as she paid her share of the bill and left the cafe.

"What's wrong with *her?*" sniffed Richelle.

Liz sighed. "She feels bad because she was the only one at school with Tom yesterday. She thinks she could have stopped him from going. Tom *does* listen to Sunny, you know. More than he listens to any of the rest of us."

"He's scared she'll beat him up if he doesn't," I joked weakly.

No one laughed.

I pulled a notebook and pen out of my bag. "Let's start making some notes," I said. "We'll see how far we get."

Liz nodded, obviously pleased that something was happening. "If it's looking good, I'll go to the gym and tell Sunny," she said. "It might make her feel better."

I turned to a fresh sheet of paper.

"Now," I said, "if you ask me, this is the big question."

At the top of the page I wrote a single word in block capitals. **WHY?**

11

The list

"That's silly, Nick," objected Richelle. "The important thing is *who's* out to get us. Not *why* they are."

"The 'why' has a good chance of leading us to the 'who'," I said.

"Good thinking," agreed Elmo, nodding. "Okay, then let's start with the most obvious. Someone's doing this — because they hate us."

I wrote "Hate" underneath the **WHY?** heading.

"But no one hates us," Richelle objected. "Except for the Work Demons, I suppose."

I wrote "Work Demons" next to "Hate."

"I don't think they actually *hate* us," said Liz doubtfully. "I think they're just jealous because we get more work than they do, and we're much better known."

"Jealousy. That's another motive," I said, and wrote it down under "Hate." Then I put "Work Demons" next to it as well.

"Money's always a motive in the movies," Richelle put in.

I put "Money" on the list.

Elmo looked doubtful. "How would anyone get money by wrecking Help-for-Hire Inc.?"

"The Work Demons would," Richelle said. "They'd get our jobs, wouldn't they?"

"They probably *are* getting our jobs, right now," Liz said gloomily. We all looked at her and she shrugged. "I forgot to tell you, because I was so worried about Tom, but Lawson's Nurseries called yesterday and canceled that fence-painting job. And we haven't had any other calls for work. I think word's spreading about us being in trouble."

"So all we've got left for next week is walking those puppies," I muttered.

"And delivering the *Pen*," Elmo reminded me.

Liz leaned her elbow on the table and propped her chin on her hand. "Delivering the *Pen* was our very first job," she said sadly. "And the way we're going, it looks like it's going to be our last. Miss Moss still hasn't been able to contact Zim, has she, Elmo?"

Elmo shook his head. "No. They took him on this walking trip. Their cell phones aren't responding because they're in a valley or something. But Mossy's left lots of messages. I'm sure he'll be in touch soon."

Liz sighed. "I wish I was walking through a beautiful New Zealand valley with nothing to think about but the weather and the scenery. No distractions, no worries, no . . ."

She broke off.

"What?" I asked impatiently.

"I was just thinking," she said slowly. "Maybe someone

63

knows we're good at detective work, and they're doing this to us so we'll be distracted. Too busy worrying to realize what's happening right under our noses."

"Good thought!" I muttered, and wrote "Distraction" on the list.

"Yes! So, what's under our noses?" Elmo excitedly ran his fingers through his messy hair, making it even messier. "People and places we know well and see a lot of. Write these down, Nick. Our families. The *Pen*. School . . ."

"Golden Pines," Liz put in. "The Glen. Burger Joe's. This place . . ."

"The puppies," Richelle chimed in, interested at last. "Our parents' work, the streets where we live . . ."

"The gym," I added, writing fast.

"I know *nothing* about the gym," Richelle protested.

"But Sunny's there all the time," Liz said.

"Well, put down my dance class, then," sniffed Richelle.

"It's not a competition, Richelle," I snapped, but wrote down "Richelle's Dance Class" anyway. Anything for peace.

"Maybe the craft shop where I go should be on there, too," Liz said doubtfully. "And your computer place, Nick. And Tom goes to the art supplies shop."

"What about the bookshop and the library?" Elmo put in.

By this time my hand was aching. I scribbled down "bookshop" and "library" and slapped the pen down. "No more!" I announced.

"Let's go and get Sunny," Liz said, jumping up. "She'll want to hear about this."

But when we got to the gym, we couldn't find Sunny anywhere. She wasn't working out on the bars or the mat; she wasn't in the weight room. Liz checked the locker rooms and the sauna, but she wasn't there, either.

"She must have finished and gone home already," Elmo said, as we walked back to the reception area.

Liz shook her head. "She couldn't have. Not so soon."

"Lost someone?" called the guy behind the reception desk. He was one of those peppy, incredibly fit-looking types I can't stand. He grinned, showing a double row of gleaming white teeth, and Liz and Richelle smiled back in the most sickening way.

"Pull yourselves together, girls," I muttered as we walked over to him, but they took no notice.

"Actually, we were looking for a friend," Richelle said, leaning on the desk and fluttering her eyelashes. "Sunny Chan. You probably wouldn't know her, but she's small, and she was wearing a green —"

"Oh, I know Sunny," the guy interrupted. "Everyone here knows Sunny. Hey, what a star." He looked us all up and down as if he was wondering how Star Sunny could have a bunch of flabby losers for friends.

Richelle's smile lost some of its gleam and she stopped fluttering her eyelashes. I snickered to myself.

"She said she was coming here," Liz said determinedly.

The guy shook his head. "She hasn't been in today," he said positively. "I've been at the desk since six."

"Oh. Well, thanks." Liz backed away from the counter, looking puzzled, and we all trailed outside again.

Elmo breathed in great gulps of air. "That place makes me nervous," he muttered. "It smells of . . . of health."

I laughed, but Liz was looking worried. "I can't understand it," she said. "Where's Sunny?"

I pulled out my cell phone and dialed Sunny's number. One of her sisters answered.

"Ah . . . it's Nick," I said. "Is Sunny there, please?"

"Hi, Nick," said the voice brightly. "This is Penny. Sunny's not home. I thought she was with you. Hold on."

She turned away from the phone and said something in Cantonese. Another voice answered.

"Grandmother's here," Penny said. "She says Sunny said she was going to the gym this morning after the paper run. Why don't you try there?"

"Oh, right, thanks," I said, and hung up. There was a sinking feeling in my stomach.

"She's not at home," Liz said flatly.

I shook my head. "Or at her grandmother's, either. They think she's at the gym."

"Well, she's not!" exclaimed Richelle impatiently. "So where is she?"

Liz, Elmo, and I looked at one another.

"Yes," Liz whispered. "Where is she?"

12

Cold trail

We walked back to the *Pen* office. It was hard to know what to do. Sunny might have just wanted to be alone. She might turn up at any moment. On the other hand . . .

"She was so upset at the cafe," Liz said miserably. "She was so worried about Tom. What if . . . ?"

"You think she might have decided to go after him?" asked Elmo hesitantly. "To the shore?"

Richelle shook her head. "She wouldn't."

"She might," I said. "That girl hates sitting around doing nothing."

"But Sunny would never hitch a ride," said Liz positively. "She always says how stupid and dangerous it is."

"She had her *Pen* delivery money," I reminded her. "She could have taken a bus."

Liz gritted her teeth. "All right," she said. "All right. So we'll go to the bus station and ask. If they don't remember seeing her, we're no worse off. If they *do* remember seeing her . . ."

Her voice trailed off. She didn't want to think about what that would mean.

✹

The bus station was much noisier and busier than I'd expected. People were standing around everywhere with their bags, chattering and laughing, looking at their watches, buying last-minute goodies from the vending machines. There were lots of kids running around.

Of course! I realized dimly. It was the first day of school vacation. I'd never felt less in a vacation mood.

There were long lines at all the ticket counters. The people behind the counters were working frantically.

"No one's going to remember selling one ticket to one girl in this mess," Richelle said crossly.

But I was thinking fast.

"This morning's buses were probably fully booked weeks ago because of the school vacation," I told the others. "If Sunny wanted a seat on a bus, she would have had to hang around hoping that someone who *did* have a ticket didn't turn up."

In one corner of the big room there was a counter with a sign that read STANDBY. A few people were huddled together on benches there, reading or just looking bored.

We hurried over to them.

"Excuse me," said Liz loudly.

They looked up hopefully. Maybe they thought she was going to tell them that a whole bunch of bus seats had suddenly become available and their long wait was over. If so, they were disappointed.

"Could you tell us if a small, Asian-American teenage girl

68

in dark green track pants and top has been here?" Liz asked. "Waiting for a ticket on a bus going south?"

Most people shook their heads, their faces blank or irritated. But a thin guy with a straggly beard and glasses nodded. "Yeah," he drawled. "Little yellow backpack, hair tied back in, like, a ponytail, right?"

"Right," said Liz in a small voice.

"She was going the same way as me. Got here just before me," the guy yawned. "About an hour ago. She had the luck. Bus was just leaving. One spare seat. She got it."

We thanked him and moved away. Liz was almost crying. Elmo patted her shoulder awkwardly, trying to make her feel better, but I could have told him nothing was going to do that. Sunny was Liz's best friend, and Sunny had run out on us without saying a word — to her, or anyone else.

I felt pretty let down myself. Tom going was one thing. Sunny going was something else.

And Richelle was furious. "How could she *do* that?" she stormed, stamping her foot. "Without saying a single word? Now we're going to have to tell her mother and the police and *everything*!"

"It's all that idiot Moysten's fault," I muttered. "She wouldn't have gone if *he* hadn't."

Elmo was concentrating on Liz. "Liz, we'll go over to the information booth and see if they'll tell us exactly which bus she got on, and how far she was —"

"NO!" shouted Liz angrily, cutting him off mid-sentence. Then she glanced at him, saw how shocked and hurt he looked, and made a face.

"I'm sorry, Elmo. I really am. I didn't mean to bite your head off," she murmured. "It's just — I don't think we ought to find out any more. The more we know about where she went, the more we're going to have to tell Dr. Chan. And I just don't want . . ."

"You don't want to get Sunny in any more trouble than you have to," Elmo finished for her. "Yeah. I understand that."

She looked at him gratefully and nodded.

"Dr. Chan will have to tell the police," Richelle put in tightly. "And I just can't imagine what *they'll* think about this, can you?"

I sighed. Unfortunately, I could.

We went to Dr. Chan's office, got in to see her, and told her what had happened. She seemed to take the news as calmly as she takes everything, but she was on the phone with the cops so fast that we knew she wasn't feeling as calm as she looked.

When she hung up she turned to us. "The police will organize with the bus company to contact the bus driver directly," she said quietly. "When they're sure Sunny's on board, they'll have the bus stopped."

She spent the next couple of minutes organizing for the rest of her patients to be seen by one of the other doctors in her office, then we all went back to her place.

About five minutes after we got there, Greta Vortek and the big, red-haired officer who'd had me by the arm on Parker Place turned up. They took us quickly through everything that had happened that morning. Then Greta went off with Dr. Chan to call for news of Sunny, and we were left with the red-haired guy, whose name had turned out to be Wildman.

Wildman looked around at us all for one long minute. Then he leaned forward, put his enormous hands on his knees, and said something that made me go cold all over.

"So, two of your friends have run out on you now," he rumbled. "Too scared to go to court. Doesn't look good, does it? Feel like changing your story yet?"

He was looking at Richelle in particular. He probably thought she'd be the easiest one of us to bully. His mistake.

"We can't change our story, because we told you the truth!" Richelle snapped, looking outraged. "You can't ask us to *lie*. And you can't blame us just because Tom and Sunny are being idiotic, either!"

Officer Wildman sighed deeply and shook his head.

"Sunny hasn't gone because she's scared," Liz spoke up, her voice trembling a bit. "I told you before. I'm sure she's gone to find Tom."

"I don't know how she's going to do that," Wildman drawled. "We're not having any luck. His dad down at the shore thinks he's not there."

He stroked his chin thoughtfully. "Mind you," he said, watching to see how we reacted, "we had an interesting report in this morning. Young man answering the description stole some chocolate bars from a shop down that way yesterday."

I kept my face absolutely still. As far as I knew Tom had

never stolen a thing in his life. But if he was hungry and didn't have any money . . . and he never could resist chocolate.

"The woman at the counter saw him, and yelled," Officer Wildman went on. "But the shop was full of people out of a tourist bus at the time, and he zipped out through the crowd and got away."

Liz gave a smothered gasp — whether of relief or horror I didn't know. Wildman glanced at her sharply.

"Later on, about five miles out of town, the same tourists going along in their bus saw him again," he said. "Sitting at the side of the road, eating one of the chocolate bars and sketching a broken-down old farmhouse. Bus driver reported it but by the time the police got there he was gone."

You fool, Tom, I thought savagely. *You run for it. You steal stuff. Then you sit around eating it in plain view because you see something you want to draw.*

It was so typical.

Greta and Dr. Chan came back into the room. Dr. Chan looked more serious than I'd ever seen her — as though she'd had very bad news.

Liz jumped up and ran over to her. "What's happened?" she exclaimed. "Is Sunny on the bus?"

Dr. Chan touched her arm gently. "Sunny *was* on the bus, Liz," she murmured. "The driver recognized her description immediately. But she's not on it anymore. The bus makes several stops along its route. Sunny got off at Clifton about half an hour ago."

"But why? Why would she do that?" Liz asked, bewildered.

"The stop is opposite the Clifton railway station," Greta put in, speaking more to Officer Wildman than to us. "The bus driver saw Sunny jogging into the station, but whether she actually intended to catch a train or not he has no idea. She could just have been taking precautions against being traced."

Wildman sighed again, even more heavily than before. "She knows exactly where she's going, I'd say. That means the boy made contact with her. Told her where he was." He turned to us, scowling.

"And you kids keep telling me you're as innocent as babies," he drawled. "Well, if you ask me, you've got a funny way of showing it."

13

More shocks

Greta and Wildman drove Liz, Elmo, Richelle, and me home.
They didn't just drop us off at the gate, either. They escorted us
right to the door and handed us over to our parents — or, in
Elmo's case, to Miss Moss at the *Pen*. At least while they were
in charge of us, they were taking no chances we'd run off like
Sunny and Tom had.

Some chance. When I saw Mom's face I knew that if I didn't
explain all this really carefully, I'd be lucky to get to go to the
mailbox on my own for the next few weeks.

So I got her to sit down and told her that the police thought
Tom had contacted Sunny and she'd gone after him to bring
him back. I downplayed some of the details and I completely left
out the part about Tom stealing candy bars. That would have
only complicated things.

Luckily, Dad had gone away on business and wouldn't be
back until the next day. That suited me. Liz, Richelle, Elmo, and
I were supposed to be walking the puppies first thing in the
morning. Dad wouldn't have been as easy to calm down as Mom.
He probably would have told me I couldn't go out.

Not that I loved walking the dogs. But I wanted an excuse to see the gang. We had to start working through the list we'd made at the Black Cat as soon as possible. There were only four of us to do it, now, and there was a lot of ground to cover.

Mom went to bed early that night, and I went to my room soon after that. I wanted a chance to think, and I find I think better in my own room than anywhere else.

I took the list out of my pocket and flattened it out on my desk. Then I sat down and studied it. It made strange reading.

WHY?

Hate — Work Demons

Jealousy — Work Demons

Money — Work Demons

Distraction — ?????

Under "Distraction" was the list of people and places we had to check out. Tomorrow, I decided, we'd divide them between ourselves. "Distraction" still seemed to me the most likely of all the motives on the list.

I doubted that the Work Demons were responsible for all this. They might have written up the graffiti, they might have started the fire, but I didn't think they'd beat up an old woman. They were bullies, but they hadn't gotten to that stage yet. More important, I didn't see how the Work Demons could have blackmailed anyone into claiming they'd seen us. They didn't have the brains for that.

And whoever was responsible for framing us had brains. The whole thing had been very well organized. Twice, phoney job appointments had lured us to places where crimes had occurred. The other time, a crime was planned near a place where we went after school every week. That meant that someone had been watching us. Someone knew what our routines were.

It was a really nasty thought. I jumped up and started getting ready for bed, telling myself to calm down. It had been a big day. I needed sleep.

But even after a hot shower I still felt jittery. In the end I decided to make myself some warm milk — not my favorite drink, but it had helped me to sleep in the past.

I got to the kitchen just in time to catch the phone on its first ring.

What now? I thought, with a stab of panic. But I was relieved when I heard the voice at the other end of the phone. It was only Liz's mother. "Nick, I'm terribly sorry to be calling at this time of night —" she began.

"That's okay, Mrs. Free," I said. "I was up."

I was so relieved that I wasn't thinking straight. I wasn't prepared for what came next. So it hit me like a punch in the stomach.

"Nick," Mrs. Free said, her voice trembling a bit. "Is Liz with you?"

I swallowed. "No," I said.

"Have you seen her tonight?"

"No, Mrs. Free."

There was silence. Then there was a muffled sound, like a choked-off sob, and when a voice came back on the line it was Liz's dad.

"Did Elizabeth say anything to you about going anywhere tonight, Nick?" he asked. "Please tell the absolute truth." He sounded stern, as though he thought I might lie.

"She didn't say anything," I said. "But Richelle might know —" My heart was thudding like a drum in my chest.

"Richelle doesn't. Or says she doesn't," he interrupted. "Elmo's phone isn't answering."

"What happened?" I managed to ask.

"We've just come home to find she's not here. Her little brother is staying with his grandmother for a few days, so she was alone in the house. She seems to have decided to take advantage of that."

I'd never heard Mr. Free sound so angry. He's really easygoing.

"I'll hang up now, Nick. If you hear from Elizabeth, please ask her to call home. Her mother is very concerned."

He broke the connection while I was still saying good-bye. I stared at the receiver, then put it down. Mr. Free was angry because he was worried. Very worried.

And I could understand why. Of all of us, Liz was the one you'd least expect to sneak out at night. And it was nearly midnight. Where was she?

Elmo might know, I though. Liz could have called him if she'd wanted to talk about something she was worried about. For some reason she trusted Elmo's judgment more than she trusted anyone else's — even Sunny's.

I dialed Elmo's number. I knew he had to be there, whatever Liz's dad said. He'd been up most of last night. He was probably sleeping and hadn't heard the phone.

Sorry, Elmo. *Wakey-wakey*, I thought, as I waited. But the phone didn't answer.

I tried again. *Ring-ring. Ring-ring.* Come on, Elmo! Finally, after three tries, I gave up.

No one could sleep through all that, I thought. *He really must be out. And maybe Liz is with him. Where could they be?*

I tried the *Pen* office. But all I got was the answering machine.

There was nothing more I could do and by this time it was way after midnight. Suddenly I felt completely exhausted. Totally forgetting about the warm milk, I turned off the lights and wandered back to my room like a sleepwalker. I don't even remember getting into bed. I must have been asleep before my head hit the pillow.

I woke up early, got dressed, and crept out of the house before Mom was awake. If I saw her I'd have to tell her about Mrs. Free's phone call, and I didn't want to do that. I left a note on the fridge telling her I'd be back in an hour or two. Then I went to the diner and killed a bit of time while I had breakfast.

When I left, it was still half dark. The sun had risen, but it was covered in clouds. It looked as though it might rain any minute. The weather matched my mood.

There was no one waiting outside the puppies' house. I told myself this was to be expected. I was a bit early. Tom and Sunny wouldn't be here, anyway, of course. And Liz's father probably wouldn't let her come, either.

Looking back on it, I think I knew all along that I was kidding myself. I just couldn't face any more problems, so I was pretending they didn't exist. But when Richelle's father's car drew up and Richelle got out looking miserable, I couldn't pretend anymore.

Richelle waited till her father drove away, then walked over to me.

"Dad didn't want me to come," she said, her voice quavering. "But I said I had to. He's coming back to pick me up in an hour."

"Liz didn't come back, did she?" I asked flatly.

She shook her head and bit her lip. "We called Mrs. Free first thing. The police were there. And Miss Moss."

"Miss Moss?" My stomach was churning.

"Elmo's gone, too," Richelle whispered. "His bed hasn't been slept in. Miss Moss checked." Tears welled up in her eyes and started spilling over and rolling down her cheeks. I put my arm around her.

"Oh, Nick," she sobbed. "I don't know what's going on!"

She wasn't the only one.

14

Clouds gather

After a few minutes, when Richelle was feeling better, we collected the puppies and hurried them down to the park. I took Happy, Sneezy, Grumpy, and Bashful; Richelle took Dopey, Sleepy, and Doc. They dragged us along, crisscrossing one another all the way and tangling their leashes in the most hopeless mess.

The dewy grass of the park saved our lives again. Once we reached that, they all stopped, sniffed, then started walking much more slowly. They didn't like getting their feet wet any more than Richelle and I did.

The park was dull and shadowy and the clouds hung low over our heads. There was no one else around. We walked slowly, talking.

"Liz's parents must be just about frantic by now — especially her mother," I said.

Richelle nodded, picking her way across the grass. "Well, at least they know Liz was still okay at eleven-thirty last night, because that's when the woman saw her and Elmo on the train," she said.

I stopped. "What?!" I yelled. "What woman? What train?"

Richelle blinked at me. "Didn't I tell you?" she asked.

"No!" I exploded.

"Well, there's no need to shout," Richelle said huffily, and walked on.

To tell the truth, it was a relief to have her acting normal again. I ran to catch up.

"Sorry. I was just surprised," I said.

Richelle shook back her hair and smoothed it, making me wait. "This woman saw Liz and Elmo on the train," she said at last. "She noticed them because there weren't many other people in the train car. Liz was knitting, and Elmo was doing a crossword. They got off at Rockville, and —"

"Rockville!?" I exploded again.

"And when the woman got off herself at the next stop," said Richelle, raising her voice and looking severely at me, "she went past the seat where they'd been sitting and saw Liz's wallet lying on the seat. It must have fallen out of her bag. Liz *never* packs her bag properly. It's just lucky someone honest found it or it never would have been handed in, and Mrs. Free would never have known —"

I couldn't help myself. "What were Liz and Elmo doing on a train to Rockville?" I interrupted.

Richelle stamped her foot. "How should I know, Nick? All I know is, they were there."

"Sunny must have called up Liz and arranged a meeting place," I said, thinking it through. "And Liz must have called Elmo. She wouldn't have wanted to travel alone at night."

Richelle lifted her chin and tossed her head. "Liz would have known there was no point asking *me* to go with her," she said in a high voice. "She'd have known that I wouldn't *dream* of doing anything so *stupid*."

But I could see she was hurt because Liz hadn't contacted her. They'd been friends since preschool.

"You and I were both with our parents last night, Richelle," I reminded her. "It would have been hard for us to get out. But Elmo was home alone. I'd say that was the reason —"

"Oh, *yes*! Of *course*! I hadn't thought of that!" Richelle actually smiled. Then her face fell again. "But now she's gone, Nick. And Elmo's gone. We're the only ones left."

"Yeah," I said gloomily. "That'll look good in court."

"Oh, don't be silly," Richelle snapped. "We're completely innocent and *we* haven't run away. It's the others you should be worrying about."

I didn't even try to argue with her. "It's going to be much harder now to find out who did this to us." I said instead. "Checking out the list —"

Richelle flapped her hands impatiently. "Nick, we can't possibly do it with just the two of us," she said.

"We have to try, though, don't we?" I knew I had to persuade her.

She shrugged.

I pulled the list out of my pocket. "Just start by talking to your mom and dad," I begged. "Find out if anything strange is happening on our street or at your dad's lumberyard. And what about your dance class?"

82

"I don't usually go on Fridays," she said sulkily.

"Richelle, *please!*" I exclaimed. "It's only two weeks till we go to court!"

Richelle glanced at me and her face changed. I think I must have looked desperate. "Well, if you really, *really* think it will help . . ." she murmured after a moment.

I nodded, very relieved.

We walked back toward the road. As we got nearer, we could see that there was a dark blue car drawn up close to the edge of the park. Two big guys in gray suits were sitting inside it. One was holding a newspaper in front of his face. The other seemed to be asleep.

"They look exactly like plainclothes policemen on TV," giggled Richelle.

"I'd say that's just what they are," I whispered back. "And they're watching us."

Richelle went pink with anger. "That's . . . an invasion of privacy! Here!" She thrust Dopey, Sleepy, and Doc's leashes into my hand and started marching toward the blue car.

"Richelle, no!" I called out in alarm, stumbling after her while the six puppies twisted their leashes around my knees.

I don't know what would have happened if Mr. Brinkley's car hadn't come over the hill at exactly that moment. But it did. Mr. Brinkley saw us, waved, and tooted.

"Oh. There's Dad," exclaimed Richelle. "He's come back for me already. We'd better hurry."

I breathed a sigh of relief. We set off up the hill again, with Mr. Brinkley driving along beside us. I glanced back at the blue car and saw that, sure enough, it was slowly turning, getting ready to follow.

○

Mr. Brinkley insisted on driving me home, and once I got there, Ma latched on to me and absolutely refused to let me go out again. She'd just heard from Mrs. Free about Liz and Elmo running away and she was scared to death I'd do the same thing.

"C'mon, Ma," I begged her. "I just want to go to Burger Joe's. And Golden Pines. And maybe the *Pen*. I've got to talk to some people. It's important."

"Nothing is more important than that you stay here with me, where I can keep my eyes on you," Ma said firmly. "You do not go anywhere, not anywhere, until your father is home."

I used my last weapon. "Don't you trust me?" I demanded.

She looked away. "I . . . want to trust you, sweetheart . . . But . . . I do not know what to think anymore," she murmured. She pulled a tissue out of her sleeve and pressed it against her eyes.

I felt bad then. She was really upset. I put my arm around her. "Okay, okay," I muttered. "Everything'll be all right."

I made her a cup of coffee and got her settled down, then I grabbed the phone book and started looking up numbers. I could do *some* investigating, at least, by phone.

But the phone started ringing before I could call anyone. It was Miss Moss from the *Pen* office. Miss Moss is usually unflappable. But not this time. She seemed to think it was her fault that Elmo had gone.

"His father says I shouldn't blame myself, but I can't help it," she kept saying. "Perhaps I should have insisted on staying with Elmo. But I didn't *dream* he'd run away. I still can't believe it."

"So you've talked to Zim, Miss Moss?" I didn't like to interrupt, but I had the feeling she might go on for hours if I didn't.

"Yes," Miss Moss said miserably. "He called a while ago. He'd just gotten my message — my first message, that is. He wanted to speak to Elmo. Imagine how I felt, having to tell him Elmo had . . . gone."

There was silence and a sniff. It was impossible to imagine Miss Moss crying, but obviously she was.

"He caught the first available flight back, of course," she went on, after a moment. "Nick, are you absolutely *certain* you don't know where Elmo is? Or any of the others?"

I told her I *was* sure. I said if I knew I'd tell her — and anyone else who asked me, because I was so mad at Elmo and the others that I could spit. And that was the truth.

After I finally hung up, Ma said I had to call Mrs. Free. She'd promised I would, but she'd forgotten. So then I had to spend another half hour swearing to Mrs. Free that I had no idea where Liz was, either.

Then at last I was able to start making my own calls. I really worked at it, in between answering calls from other people like Tom's mom, Sunny's sister Penny, and Greta Vortek.

No one I spoke to could think of anything suspicious happening around Raven Hill — except for what was happening with Help-for-Hire Inc. The fact that four of us had taken off without a word even made people who knew us well, like the staff at Golden Pines, feel nervous.

85

By late afternoon, I slumped back in my chair feeling depressed and frustrated. I seemed to have spent the day on the phone, and all I'd gotten out of it was a sore ear and a bad feeling.

When the phone rang yet again, I didn't want to answer it. I let it ring for a long time before I finally picked up the receiver.

It was Mrs. Brinkley. And what she said made me sit up . . . fast.

"Nick!" she said in a high, panicky voice. "Is Richelle with you?"

15

And then there was one

Richelle had told her parents she wanted to go to Friday afternoon dance class. Her mother had driven her to the hall and dropped her outside. But when Mr. Brinkley went to pick her up, she wasn't waiting in the parking lot. She wasn't inside the hall, either. And never had been, according to the teacher. She hadn't gone to class at all.

The Brinkleys were just about hysterical. They called the police after talking to me. Greta Vortek went straight to see them. They told her that Richelle must have been abducted. She'd never go off on her own without telling them, they said.

But when Greta came to see me that night, it was obvious that she didn't agree. She asked me all sorts of questions about Richelle — how she'd behaved when we walked the puppies, what I thought her emotional state was like.

My own emotional state wasn't too good by then. I was so tired and frazzled that I don't think I answered any of the questions very convincingly. Greta left, looking grim.

Dad wasn't expected home until late. Mom had a terrible headache, which wasn't surprising. I got her to take some aspirin and lie down. Then I turned on the answering machine, went to my room, and lay down myself. My head wasn't aching, but it was spinning as though my brain had gotten on a merry-go-round and couldn't get off.

Richelle had deserted me — just like Tom, Sunny, Liz, and Elmo. They'd all gone and left me to face the police, the court, and everything else alone.

Had I been wrong about them all along? Was it possible that they'd been fooling me, pretending they believed someone was out to get us when all the time they were the guilty ones? Was it possible that, without me realizing it, the others had all gotten so hooked on excitement that when things got boring they created their own?

All those crimes Help-for-Hire Inc. had solved. Were they the problem?

I remember lying there, my eyes closed, trying to slow down my mind. Then, without any warning, I must have just fallen asleep.

When I woke up, it was very dark. Someone had turned off my light and covered me with a quilt. I could hear the faint sound of snoring coming from my parents' bedroom. Dad was home. I rolled over and checked the time. Two A.M.

I lay still for a moment, blinking. The spinning in my head had stopped. My mind felt perfectly clear.

More than clear. It was as though while I was asleep my

brain-computer had been quietly working away without me, sorting information, throwing away the useless stuff, homing in on the answer. All the thoughts I'd been having before seemed absurd now. Except one.

I got up, went to my desk, and switched on the reading light. I pulled out the list of motives from my pocket.

Hate.

Jealousy.

Money.

Distraction.

Now I realized that in a way they were all true. But there was one missing. The most important one. The one that tied all the rest together.

I took a pen and wrote it in.

REVENGE.

❁

Ten minutes later I was on the streets, jogging through the light, misty rain. In a lot of ways it was a stupid thing to do. Though I hadn't seen the dark blue car outside my house, it could have been there, hidden behind one of the big trees farther down the road.

But if I was right, what I had to do couldn't wait until morning. Couldn't wait for long explanations, either. And I had the advantage over anyone who was following me. I knew where I was going.

I ducked into a little alleyway, ran to the end, and then

dodged around some buildings. *Let them try to follow me down here,* I thought. I climbed a fence, felt my way through a dark little yard behind a shop, climbed another fence, then crept along the narrow lane that led to the back of the *Pen* building.

The padlock on the big roller shutter was heavy and new. But the one on the little door beside it was a different matter. I was able to open it using the crowbar I'd taken from the trunk of Dad's car. I'd often wondered why the *Pen* office wasn't robbed more often. I suppose even stupid kids realized there wasn't anything in it worth taking.

But there was something in it I wanted just now.

I closed the door after me, so that anyone walking past wouldn't realize it had been interfered with. Then I shuffled through the dark delivery bay and climbed up into the main office.

Even there, I didn't dare turn on the light. It wasn't until I got to the tiny, windowless room that was the *Pen* library that I felt safe.

In the library there were copies of every single *Pen* that had ever been printed. The oldest ones, from Elmo's grandfather's time, were bound into big leather books. One book for every year. The newer ones were in plainer binders. But again, there was one for each year.

It was the newest ones I wanted. The ones that carried the stories about Help-for-Hire Inc.

I pulled the first one down from its shelf and sat down with it at the reading table that filled the center of the room. I started leafing through until I found my starting point. Our very first ad.

HELP-FOR-HIRE INC.

Five responsible, mature teenagers will tackle any jobs around your house, garden, shop, or business. Typing OK, computer OK, children and pets OK. Raven Hill area only. Cheap hourly rate. No job too small. We'll do anything!

It still sounded good, after all this time. I sat for a moment, looking at it, remembering. Then I shook my head. I couldn't waste time feeling sentimental.

I started leafing quickly through the pages, and wherever I found a story about us, big or small, I read it, made some notes, then marked the place with a strip of paper and went on. I was sure I'd be able to finish the job before morning. If I was right, it was pretty certain that the story I was looking for would be among the early ones.

It was fascinating to read about all the old cases. I remembered them all so well. Zim had certainly given us plenty of publicity. And we'd given *him* some very good headlines.

I worked as fast as I could, scanning the news sections of each paper, then turning quickly to the next. I guess I'd been there about twenty minutes when suddenly I heard something that made the hairs on the back of my neck prickle. Someone was walking softly through the office. Coming this way!

Someone must have seen me coming in and called the police. Or maybe the security guy who patrolled this area had noticed the broken lock on the back door.

I looked wildly around the room. Nowhere to hide. But I couldn't just stay here and be caught. Not now.

Could whoever it was see the light under the door? If not, maybe there was still a chance. I'd turn off the light, then get behind the door. He'd look in, see a dark, empty room, and go on.

That was the plan. But just as I put my hand up to the switch, the door burst open and a roaring, furious figure leaped into the room, knocking me backward.

I hit the floor, twisting my leg, smashing against a table leg, yelling my head off. Then I jumped up again, ignoring the pain, determined to get away, whatever it took.

And then I saw who my attacker was.

It was Zim.

16

Danger

"I'm so sorry, Nick. But when I saw the light under the library door, I thought we had burglars and so . . . I just went for it," babbled Zim as he fussed around making coffee.

"Zim, it doesn't matter," I said for about the twelfth time. "It's my own fault. I *did* break in, so I might as well have been a burglar."

He passed me a steaming mug, and I sipped at it gratefully.

"When did you get home?" I asked.

"I haven't actually *been* home yet," he said, munching on a cookie. "I got a taxi from the airport to the police station. Richelle's gone now, I hear. To join the others, presumably."

"I guess," I said slowly. "That's what I thought last night. But now it seems . . . incredible."

He shook his head at me. "They were crazy to go. Who's going to believe they're innocent now?"

"I know," I said with feeling.

"After I'd finished with the police I felt pretty bad, so I decided to walk home," Zim went on. "Walking always helps me clear my head. I was thinking over and over, 'This is crazy. I've got to get them to come back. How can I do that?' So I thought to myself, my only chance of getting them to come back of their own accord is to assure them they're safe. I have to prove they *didn't* attack that poor old woman on Parker Place. Or set the leaves on fire. Or write that graffiti at the school."

"You believe us." A feeling of incredible gratitude swept through me.

"Of course!" said Zim, almost angrily. "You're being framed. It's obvious."

"It doesn't seem to be obvious to anyone else," I muttered. "Two plainclothes cops in a blue car were shadowing Richelle and me yesterday, waiting for us to make a break for it. They think we're criminals."

He glanced at me sideways. "Maybe it was clearer to me because I wasn't here," he said. "And in my business — well, you hear a lot of strange things. Anyway, after I'd been walking a while, it suddenly came to me. The reason behind all this. So I came straight here to check —"

"To check through our old cases," I finished for him. "Me, too."

We went back into the library, carrying our coffee and a bag of cookies. My leg was sore and I was limping. My shoulder ached, too. But I didn't want Zim to start fussing again, so I didn't say anything.

"I don't know why I didn't think of it before," I said, sitting down at the table. I helped myself to a cookie. Suddenly I was starving. "It was so obvious," I said to Zim, with my mouth full. "So obvious none of us saw it. People were talking all the time about how we'd solved all these mysteries — but that was because they thought we'd gotten hooked on the excitement and the publicity."

Zim snorted contemptuously.

I shrugged and took another cookie. "Things got so bad that even I started thinking it. Yesterday I was incredibly tired and mixed up. I fell asleep wondering if all those crimes Help-for-Hire Inc. had solved really *were* the problem. But when I woke up, I suddenly saw that idea the right way around. Sure, we'd solved a lot of crimes. But that hadn't affected us at all. The people who it *had* affected were —"

"The criminals you stopped in their tracks," Zim finished for me. "Someone's spent quite a bit of time in jail thinking about Help-for-Hire Inc. Making plans."

"Revenge," I muttered.

Zim nodded. "Of course! So let's get going. Let's work out who we're dealing with."

He threw himself down in a chair and ran his fingers through his tousled hair. For a moment he looked a lot like Elmo.

How strange, I thought. *I've never had much time for Zim. I've always thought he was slow, disorganized, impractical, a bad business-man. And maybe he is. But he's got imagination and he's willing to follow hunches. Those things are valuable, too. More valuable than anything, just at the moment.*

"Well," I said, "it has to be someone ruthless and violent. Willing to hurt an old woman just to get at us. It has to be someone well-organized, with other people he can call on for help when necessary. A man made the first fake job call. A woman made the second. It's someone who knows about us — our habits and our movements. And because of that I *think* it must be

95

someone who's been in jail for a while. Someone who's had a chance to do some research. From an old case, rather than a new one."

Zim nodded slowly. "Fair enough. Any possibilities so far?"

"The Raven Hill Gripper case," I said, looking at my notes.

Zim shook his head. "Still in jail, and not enough contacts to organize a thing like this from there," he said briefly. "Next?"

"The Phantom of the Library," I said. Again, he shook his head. "Ditto," he said.

I started reading my list more rapidly. "The Gingerbread House mystery — that criminal they call The Wolf was involved in that. Then there were those goons who kidnapped Elmo's Aunt Vivien. And that crooked real estate developer —"

"Whoa!" exclaimed Zim, holding up his hand, his eyes bright with excitement. "Back up, Nick, back up!"

"How far?" I glanced again at my notes.

"The Wolf," Zim breathed. "You destroyed a nice little scheme he had going, didn't you?"

He got up and started pacing around the little room. "The Wolf! Why didn't I think of him before?" he muttered. "He fits the profile perfectly! Ruthless, violent, well-organized, a whole network of petty criminals working for him . . . And arrogant, Nick. Incredibly arrogant. No one who ever crossed him got away with it. Except you."

"Only for a while, it seems," I drawled. "If it's him who's after us —"

Zim spun around. "We're going to the police."

"We can't do that yet!" I objected, surprised. "We're not *sure* it's The Wolf. He could still be in jail. Then we'll look like fools."

Zim frowned at me. "The Wolf could organize a thing like this from inside prison if he wanted to. And he's dangerous, Nick. Very dangerous. If he's after Help-for-Hire Inc. it's a wonder that he's been satisfied just to get you into trouble. Most of his enemies are dead. They've never been able to charge him with murder. It's always a hit-and-run accident or a fire or a fatal fall. But everyone knows who gave the orders."

When he put it like that, I wasn't going to argue. I drained my coffee, grabbed Dad's crowbar and a handful of cookies and followed him out the door.

We turned off the lights and left the building by the front entrance. To my annoyance I found my leg had gotten worse while I was sitting down. I was limping very badly.

Zim glanced at me in concern as he locked the door. "You stay here," he said. "I'll go and get the car. I'll be back in fifteen minutes."

He hurried away through the misty rain and soon disappeared around the corner. I propped myself against the closed door, huddled up in my jacket, and got ready for the wait. I wished I'd brought another cup of coffee out with me. But at least I had something to eat.

I checked out the cookies in my hand, found a coconut one, and ate it. After that there were three left. I decided to ration them. One cookie every five minutes. That way I should be finishing the last one when Zim came back.

Imagine my surprise when only about four minutes later

Zim's car came gliding around the corner. I limped to the side of the road. How had he made the trip so quickly?

There were two men in the car. As it pulled to a stop, the passenger door opened and one of them got out. I recognized him. It was one of the men who'd been sitting in the blue car down at Raven Hill Park.

He flashed a badge at me. "Senior Officer Warren," he said gruffly. "So, Nick. You gave us the slip nicely, didn't you? Lucky we decided to check this area again."

He took my arm and opened the back door of the car. "Get in," he ordered. "You've got some questions to answer down at the station."

Confused thoughts were tumbling over one another in my mind. "They *were* following me . . . I'm in trouble . . . no, I'm not, because of Zim . . . Zim's gone to get his car . . . this *is* Zim's car . . . what are the police doing in Zim's car? . . . they've stolen Zim's car . . . *these aren't police at all!*"

The grip on my arm tightened. "In you get," the voice said roughly, and pushed me toward the open car door. I heard my own voice yelling in protest. At the same time I was thinking, *All shops and businesses around here. No one will hear you.*

I was beside the car, now. Zim's new car. How would he feel when he found out it had been stolen from outside his house? In my confusion, a memory of Elmo's voice popped into my head. Elmo, being irritating, telling us all more than we wanted to know about the wonderful new car Zim had won. Telling us . . .

I was still clutching my precious cookies. They were breaking and crumbling in my fist. I opened my fingers and let the crumbs fall onto the sidewalk. Then the man's hand was on my head, pushing it down, and I was being thrust into the car, and he was clambering in beside me.

The door slammed. The car took off with a jerk and a small squeak of tires. The man beside me said pleasantly, "Just turn and face the window, will you, Nick?"

I turned. There was a quick movement behind me, a flashing explosion of pain like fireworks going off in my head . . . and then there was only blackness.

17

Action

I was inside a cupboard. The back of my head was pressed against something and it was hurting me, but I didn't dare move. Outside the cupboard, very near, a growling voice was talking. I knew that if the thing that owned the voice found me, something horrible would happen. I could almost see its long, sharp teeth, red tongue, and dripping jaws. I could almost feel its hot breath on my face. . . .

"Made nice time," the voice growled. "This little baby is a hundred times better than that gutless blue thing. I'll be sorry to dump it."

That's a funny thing for a wolf to say, I thought. Then, slowly I realized that I'd been dreaming. I wasn't in a cupboard, I was in the backseat of a car. My head hurt because I'd been hit. And there was no wolf waiting to eat me. Not yet.

But the voice was real. And the reason came to me slowly. The driver of the car was talking to the man sitting next to me.

I kept my eyes closed. I didn't make a sound. I knew that if they realized I'd woken up they might hit me again.

I listened hard. I couldn't hear any traffic noises. Just the hum of the car moving along a smooth road. So we were out of the city. On a highway somewhere.

I felt the car slow down and swing to the left. Now the road was a bit bumpier.

"How's Sleeping Beauty, Mike?" asked the driver.

I concentrated on keeping still, terrified my eyelids would flicker and give me away as Mike bent over me.

"Still in dreamland," he said, "Lucky we saw him when we did, after losing him like that, Sammy. What d'you think he was doing just standing there on the street? With a crowbar in his hand. In plain sight! The cops could have picked him up on suspicion. How stupid can you get?"

"How stupid would you have to be to cross The Wolf in the first place?" Sammy said. "Crazy, that's what you'd have to be."

The car was very warm, but suddenly I felt cold. So Zim had been right. Our enemy was The Wolf. I'd been kidnapped by The Wolf's men. And Zim had said The Wolf's enemies ended up dead.

My throat was tight. Maybe Richelle, Liz, Elmo, Sunny, and Tom hadn't run away at all. Maybe The Wolf's men had gotten them, too. Just like they'd gotten me. By pretending to be police.

If so, what had The Wolf done with them?

I could hardly breathe. *Then – no*, I thought. *I'm being stupid. They've run away. They were seen on trains, buses, hitch-hiking – and they weren't being forced. Liz was knitting, Elmo doing a crossword, Tom sketching an old farmhouse . . . They wouldn't have been doing those things if they were terrified.*

Wherever they are, they're safe, I thought.

It was weird, but that made me feel better. I might be in terrible danger myself, but at least the others were okay. Liz, Sunny, Elmo, and Tom, anyway. I wasn't so sure about Richelle.

I felt the car turn again. To the right, this time. It went for a little way over gravel, then stopped.

Mike yawned. "Six A.M.," he groaned. "The Boss won't like being woken at this hour."

"He'll have to deal with it. It's not our fault the chance came when it did, is it?" growled Sammy. "Our orders were whenever and however. Right?"

"Right." Mike yawned again. Then he nudged at me. "Wakey-wakey, Sunshine," he said.

I didn't move. He shook me, and I lolled sideways in my seat belt, a dead weight.

"You hit him too hard, you dope," growled Sammy. I felt him poking at my shoulder with a hard finger. "Boss won't like that. He wants him awake. That was the orders."

"It's not my fault. He must have one of them thin skulls," Mike whined. "Listen, he'll be okay. He's breathing all right. Let's just let him sleep it off here for a while. No need to tell anyone we're back yet, is there? No one'll be up for hours. We can sneak in the side door, have some food, relax . . ."

"I dunno," said Sammy doubtfully. "Orders are —"

"He's big. He'll be a dead weight," Mike interrupted persuasively. "And with your back, Sammy —"

"Ah, all right," Sammy said, suddenly convinced.

Mike grunted, relieved, and clambered out of the car.

"What if he wakes up while we're gone?" I heard Sammy ask.

Mike guffawed. "What if he does? He'll be hurting too much to go anywhere. And where'd he go anyhow?"

The door slammed. I heard the faint crunching of feet on gravel, then nothing.

I stayed where I was with my eyes closed, while I counted to a hundred, just in case they were hanging around to see if I was pulling a fast one.

But everything stayed quiet, and at last I decided I was safe. Cautiously, I opened my eyes.

And then I got a surprise. I was in a parking lot behind a luxury hotel! But the hotel seemed to have been built in the middle of nowhere. Flat, grassy land stretched out on either side of it as far as the eye could see.

I felt in my jacket pocket. Mike had taken my keys, my wallet, and, as I'd feared, my cell phone. I wasn't going to be able to call for help that way.

So I needed a weapon. The crowbar.

I groped around on the floor near where Mike had been sitting, and pulled the crowbar out from where it had been shoved under the seat in front. Then, clutching it, I crept out of the car and closed the door gently.

Other cars were parked in spots neatly marked by clipped hedges. Lights glowed softly over a sign at the head of a path that led to the hotel entrance.

WELCOME TO SUMMERFIELD the sign read, in flowing script. And then in smaller letters underneath: HEALTH AND BEAUTY. THE DREAM STARTS HERE.

I crouched behind one of the cars and thought. It must have

been one of those resorts where people go to lose weight or just to live a healthy life for a while. That was why it was in such an isolated area. So the visitors wouldn't be tempted to sneak into town for burgers and fries.

What was I going to do now? There were two possibilities. I could make a run for it back to the highway in the hope that a car would pick me up. Or I could get into the hotel and try to find a phone.

The choice wasn't hard to make, really. For one thing, I was sure Mike and Sammy wouldn't be gone for long. They'd soon discover I was missing, and they'd start looking. The area around the hotel was bare and flat — nowhere to hide. Running was a sure way of getting caught. Especially with a damaged leg.

And apart from that, it was quite likely that Richelle was locked up in the hotel somewhere. If I hadn't been in such a confused, tired state at the time she disappeared, I'd never have believed she'd run away. Richelle hates being uncomfortable, she hates trains and buses. And besides, she wasn't afraid of going to court. She'd always assumed we'd be found not guilty.

The path from the parking lot led to a pair of glass doors that must have been the back entrance to the hotel. There was a light glowing inside. Probably that door was locked, or guarded, at night.

But Mike had talked about a side door. I edged across the gravel, keeping behind the cars and hedges. When I'd reached a point opposite the side of the hotel I left the parking lot and limped quickly to the shelter of the building.

The door I was looking for wasn't far from the corner, at the end of a row of plastic garbage cans. I pressed my ear against it and listened carefully. I couldn't hear anything. Gently I twisted the knob and eased open the door.

I found myself standing in a brilliantly lit kitchen — all shining white tiles and glimmering stainless steel. There were crumbs, half a loaf of bread, some eggs, and a couple of knives lying on a chopping board on one of the benches. There was also the smell of coffee. Mike and Sammy had already helped themselves to breakfast.

I crept to the swinging doors that I knew must lead to the dining room and listened, but heard no voices. They must have taken their food away to eat.

I slipped through the doors, crossed the dim, deserted room where white-covered tables were set for breakfast, and peered into the hallway beyond. I saw the back entrance to the right. To the left was an elevator and a staircase that led up to the higher floors and down to the basement. There was no sign of anyone. And no sound.

Except . . . I concentrated for a couple of seconds. Yes, I was right. Faint, very faint — voices. Floating up the stairs from the floor below me. Voices, and once, twice — a high-pitched scream.

I didn't even think about it. I went for the stairs and ran silently down to the basement floor. It was dim; a long, broad hallway with doors set into the wall here and there. I could see light shining through a glass panel in one of the doors near the end. I listened, my skin crawling.

There was another shriek and some high-pitched laughter. The sounds were coming from behind the lighted door. I crept along to it, my heart thudding, and peered through the glass panel, terrified of what I was going to see.

What I saw was a huge indoor swimming pool. The clear blue water was rippling and splashing. And at the far end, playing around in it — swimming, jumping, pushing at each other, having a really good time — were Tom, Liz, Sunny, Elmo, and Richelle.

I was so stunned and furious that for a second I just couldn't move. Which was lucky, because just as I recovered, just as I was about to bang open the door and confront them, a sixth figure I hadn't noticed got up from one of plastic chairs that were scattered around the pool.

And the sixth figure was me.

18

In the nick of time

I held on to the door, gaping, unable to believe my own eyes. Was I going crazy?

But the next moment I realized what I was seeing. The sixth figure, now throwing down his towel and getting ready to dive into the pool with the others, *looked* like me. But he wasn't me. Well, of course he wasn't!

And the friendly-looking brown-haired girl who was laughing up at him looked like Liz. But she wasn't Liz. And the beautiful girl with the cloud of long, fair hair wasn't Richelle. The tall, skinny guy getting ready to splash her again wasn't Tom. The small, trim, Asian-American girl in the green swimsuit wasn't Sunny. And that guy talking to her, the guy with freckles and a mop of dripping, curly red hair, wasn't Elmo.

But from a distance, how could anyone who didn't know us well tell the difference?

I stared, fascinated. Here in front of me was the answer to the whole mystery. The Wolf hadn't blackmailed Fenelli and the others to say they'd seen us committing crimes. He'd done something even more amazing than that.

He'd found six kids who looked so like us that any eyewitness would be fooled. He'd used our doubles to convince everyone that Help-for-Hire Inc. had gone bad. Clothes weren't a problem. All the crimes were committed while we were in school uniform, easy to copy. And afterward . . .

Suddenly, the whole, awful plan came crashing in on me. I backed away from the door, my hands cold and my heart pounding in my chest.

Afterward, when the date of our court appearance had been set, he'd had us kidnapped, one by one, and gotten his look-alikes to dress in our clothes and show themselves on buses, trains, hitch-hiking. Acting like us, looking like us. Like us running away.

And that could only mean one thing. The Wolf planned for the Help-for-Hire gang never to get back to Raven Hill. The look-alikes would be paid off, then they'd quietly separate and go back to whatever they were doing before The Wolf employed them. The police, our parents — everyone — would think we'd gone into hiding somewhere.

And meanwhile, our *true* fates would have been left in the hands of The Wolf. He would have had his revenge. But it would be his secret. No one would ever suspect him.

The soft *ting* of the elevator bell broke into my thoughts like a fire alarm. Someone was coming! I looked wildly around. At the end of the hallway was a door marked DANGER. STAFF ONLY. I leaped for it, praying it wasn't locked.

It wasn't. I made it into cover just as the elevator doors opened, and I huddled in the thick, black dark beyond the door, shivering with nervous tension.

I couldn't hear anything. The roar of machinery working

very near me drowned out all other sounds. The air-conditioning unit, maybe, I thought. The swimming pool filter. Who knew? But whatever, this room's soundproofing was very good. I hadn't been able to hear any of this racket from the hallway.

I was desperate to open the door a crack so as to see who had come down in the elevator and where they were. But I didn't dare move. And then, just as I felt I couldn't stand the tension anymore, the door was pushed open and the light went on.

After the pitch-blackness, the light was blinding. I scrambled clumsily back behind the door as it opened. If it hadn't been for the roar of the machinery, the guy who was coming through the door would have heard me for sure.

But he didn't hear me. And he didn't look behind him. The door swung shut by itself as he moved across the little room, heading for some narrow wooden stairs in one corner. He was carrying a big orange jug of water and a plastic bag of bread rolls.

And when I saw that, my heart leaped. Why bring food and water to a place like this? There was only one reason that I could think of. Even a team of pet rats couldn't eat that much bread at a sitting.

The man was clambering down the stairs now, grunting irritably to himself. I left my place by the door and peered cautiously over the rail as he reached the bottom and trudged on, out of sight.

I followed. My leg must have still been hurting, but I can't remember even noticing it. All I could think about was keeping as quiet as I could, not falling down the stairs, which were flimsy and steep as a ladder, and keeping the man in sight.

He'd turned on another light. We were walking through the basement, on a brick floor. The roof was very low, and I had to duck my head to avoid hitting the huge beams of wood that supported the floor above. The air smelled damp and musty.

At the end of the bricked space was a wall with one metal door, padlocked on the outside. The man put down his jug and the rolls, then stretched up to a shelf above the door and pulled down a flashlight and a key.

I crouched in a dark corner as he undid the padlock, switched on the flashlight, and picked up the jug and the plastic bag. The crowbar was heavy in my hand. I considered running up behind him and whacking him over the head with it. That would put him out cold. But the people who'd sent him down here would start to wonder why he didn't come back. They'd come down to investigate.

Better to wait, I thought, and watched as he heaved the door open.

Beyond the door there was deep blackness and no sound that I could hear over the dull roaring from the machine room. The man went into the darkness, the flashlight beam making a circle of light at his feet. The door swung shut behind him.

It was agony just waiting there, not knowing what was happening inside the room or what was in there. But I knew I couldn't risk doing anything else.

It seemed to be hours, but it was probably only about ten minutes before the man came back through the door. An empty jug, green this time, swung loosely from his hand. He switched off the flashlight and put it back on the shelf. Then he padlocked the door again and put the key away with the flashlight.

Then, sighing and grumbling to himself, he trudged back toward the stairs. I held my breath as he passed, terrified that he'd spot me. But he didn't stop or look around, and after a moment the basement light went off. Then I heard feet clumping up the wooden stairs. And then, at last, the glow of light from the machine room upstairs disappeared. The man had gone.

It was so dark that I had to feel my way to the metal door. I stretched up and felt for the flashlight and the key. There they both were, cold under my fingers.

My hands were shaking. I tried to hold them steady as I switched on the flashlight, stuck the key in the padlock, and turned it.

The padlock came loose. I pushed open the door and shone the flashlight into the room — across a bare floor, past a bare brick wall, on to another wall.

And then five pale faces were caught in the light. I saw tangled hair, gagged mouths, dark circles under blinking eyes . . .

Tom, Sunny, Liz, Elmo, Richelle.

19

Together again

I untied them, my hands trembling. I pulled the stifling gags away. And then we were running out of the basement and up the flimsy stairs. Then, in the machine room, we talked.

We all wanted to get out, and get out quickly. But there was a big snag. By now, Mike and Sammy would have discovered that I wasn't in the car. They'd be looking for me. They'd be panicky, terrified that The Wolf would find out they'd blown it. We couldn't risk going outside. We had to hide and play for time.

"There's only one answer," I said. "They'll keep combing the hotel till they catch me. So we'll have to let them do it."

"No!" Liz exclaimed, clutching my arm. "No way!"

And Richelle shook her head decidedly. "They keep you in the dark, Nick. They only give you bread to eat and water to drink. And when they take you to the bathroom they *stand outside* the whole time, and bang on the door if you take too long. It's *disgusting!*"

"You've hardly been here any time, Richelle. I've been here for days," growled Tom. "How do you think I feel?"

"For goodness' sake!" exclaimed Liz. "Don't argue now! But,

Nick, for your idea to work — I mean, if they caught you — they'd take you down there into the basement to lock you in with us. And then they'd find out we weren't there."

I smiled. "You haven't heard the rest of the idea," I said.

We made our plans, and then we carried them out. We took a risk, moving out into the hallway and ambushing our doubles as they left the swimming pool, looking forward to a nice, leisurely breakfast. But no one heard them yell, and alone they had no chance. They were just kids who looked like us. We were the real thing, and we were fighting for our lives.

We each took care of our own double. It was weird — like fighting your own shadow. We wrestled them through the machine room, down to the basement. We made them switch clothes with us. Then we made all of them, except the one who looked like me, sit down where the others had been. We gagged them and tied them up. Then we locked the door and left them. And not even Liz protested. Even she knew that it was time to be ruthless.

We dragged my double back upstairs with us.

"Who are you? What do you want?" he gibbered.

I looked at him in disgust. Now that I looked at him closely I couldn't imagine how anyone could really have thought he was me. His black hair was flopping over his face, and his face was twisted with fear.

"He looks so like you, Nick. It's amazing!" murmured Elmo, which annoyed me a lot.

"Tell us what you know!" I said to the phoney.

"It was just a job," he stammered, his eyes darting everywhere, especially at me. "Some joke or bet or something. We — the others and me — we had to act the parts of some kids who were going bad. You know — write some stuff on a wall, set fire to a pile of leaves, run out of a backyard — "

"And beat up a poor old lady!" exclaimed Liz.

He stared at her, wild-eyed. "We never beat up anybody!" he yelled.

"The Wolf probably organized that attack himself," Elmo said quietly. "He just got the doubles to gather in the backyard of the house on Parker Place and run so the neighbor would see them."

"I didn't know anyone got hurt inside that house!" my double mumbled. "Honest!"

For a moment I wavered. But then I remembered Mike hitting me on the head, and the faces of my friends in that dark basement, and I felt strong and ruthless again.

"Out!" I said to him.

We marched through the door. Past the swimming pool, up the stairs, toward the dining room.

And then we heard voices. Desperate voices.

"We never should have left him!" That was Sammy. Angry. "Why'd I let you talk me into it? Where is he?"

"Well, he's not on the highway, is he? And he's not wandering around the grounds. So he's here. We'll find him and the Boss won't know anything about it, right?" That was Mike. Panicky.

They came closer. Closer. I pushed my double violently forward, so he yelled and stumbled.

"Hear that?" I heard Mike shout.

"Go!" I hissed at the others.

And then we were gone, up the stairs this time. Up, up, until we were at the next floor.

And meanwhile, down below, my double was stumbling to his feet, and Mike and Sammy were pouncing on him, gleeful and triumphant.

"I'm not the one you want!" I heard my double screeching. "It's not me! It's the other one!"

"That knock on the head didn't do you any good, did it, Sunshine?" said Sammy. "Never mind, you'll cool down where we're taking you. Right, Mike?"

"Right," said Mike. "Down we go."

And they took him away.

"What now?" Liz whispered, after we'd waited a few minutes.

"We're wearing the others' clothes," grinned Tom. "So all we have to do is act like them and we've got the run of the place. Let's get some breakfast."

"We should just find a quiet room and stay there," Sunny frowned at him. "It shouldn't be too long. If what Elmo said about Zim's car is true —"

"Of course it is!" exclaimed Elmo, insulted.

"*Ssh!*" Tom hissed.

The elevator bell was quietly *ting*-ing two floors down. We heard the doors rolling open. Someone was following Mike and Sammy to the basement.

Carefully, we crept down and peered over the stair rails. We saw a huge figure in gray trousers and a blue-and-white patterned shirt lumbering along the hallway. A man was walking on one side of him, a woman the other.

I looked at the big man and shivered. It was a long time since I'd seen The Wolf, but I remembered those piggy little eyes peering from pouches of fat, those bristly black eyebrows and those huge, red hands like thick pieces of steak. Who could forget them?

"So," the woman was saying in a clipped, dry voice, "those idiots pulled it off. Finally."

The man snickered. "What now?"

The Wolf spread his huge hands. "Now our young guests can be disposed of. As soon as I have seen them. The apparatus is set up. I simply wanted them to be together. To know what was happening to them. To know why. That was what I wanted. And that is what will happen."

Neither of the others said anything else. They all just walked on toward the machine-room door.

We stood where we were, looking down, paralyzed.

"He's going to hurt them," Tom said in a strangled voice. "We can't just hide here and let —"

"He was going to hurt *us*, Tom," Richelle interrupted in a high voice. "Would you rather it was us down there?"

"The Wolf's not stupid like Mike and Sammy," I said. "He'll realize the kids in the cellar aren't us."

"What if he doesn't?" Liz demanded.

"We can't risk it," Elmo said firmly.

Sunny, Richelle, and I looked at one another.

"I don't think they knew what they were doing," Sunny said finally.

"That's right. They were just offered work and a lot of money, and took it. It could have been us," hissed Tom.

"No, it couldn't! We wouldn't have done the things they did," Richelle protested.

"Maybe not. But they don't deserve to suffer like this," said Elmo.

He was right. Of course he was. We all knew it.

"We've got a bit of time," I said. "From what he said, he's just going down there to gloat. Whatever he's planning to do to them, it won't happen until after he comes back. He talked about an apparatus. He'll have to give the order to set it going."

"There's a piece of rubber pipe sticking through the wall right up high, above where our heads were," Elmos said. "I'd say he's planning to fill the basement with gas. Maybe with car exhaust. I think there's an underground parking lot on the other side of the wall."

We were silent for a moment, thinking about the terror of the six kids we'd left tied up in that dark basement. If The Wolf didn't realize he'd been tricked, they were doomed. If he *did* realize it, we were in big trouble. He'd have the hotel searched until we were found.

"We've got to stop him from getting back to the main part of the hotel," I said aloud. "Keep him down in the basement until . . ."

My voice trailed off, and I saw Elmo crossing his fingers.

I looked at the crowbar in my hand. It had been very handy so far. It would make a good weapon. But could it match a gun? I didn't think so.

"He's huge. Maybe he'll get stuck halfway down those narrow steps," Tom joked feebly. "Or they'll fall down under his weight."

I glanced at him quickly and grinned. He looked surprised. I don't usually laugh at his jokes.

"Nick's got an idea," said Richelle knowingly.

I nodded and held up the crowbar.

20

End game

What we had to do didn't take too long. The first part, getting down to the basement and levering the bottom of the little wooden staircase up so the nails that held it down to the floor came loose, was scary. I kept thinking The Wolf would come back from the basement before I'd finished.

But he didn't come and, as I'd hoped, the roar of the machinery from the room above blocked the noise. I ran up the steps again, feeling relieved, and did the same job on the nails that fastened the top to the machine-room floor.

After that, the staircase wasn't attached to anything, either at the top or at the bottom. It was just like a giant ladder. And so, working together, we were able to heave it up until it was lying on the floor besides us.

We were still congratulating ourselves when there was an angry shout from below. We looked down the hole where the stairs had been. The Wolf was standing there, purple in the face with shock and rage. The man and the woman beside him were both spluttering, blinking at the place where the stairs had been as though they expected them to suddenly reappear.

"I told you those kids weren't the right ones!" The Wolf howled. "Those fools! Those idiots! Now we're trapped down here."

I couldn't resist it. I bent down and poked my head over the gap in the floor so he could see me.

"Yeah. Hope you enjoy it, Wolf," I drawled. "My friends had a great time."

The Wolf bared his teeth and clenched his fists. The veins in his forehead seemed to swell. "You — you —" he choked, reaching into his jacket pocket.

I jerked back quickly from the edge and backed away, fast. He might have been armed.

The shouts from the basement followed us through the machine room. But out in the hallway, with the door shut safely behind us, we couldn't hear a thing.

We walked back up the stairs to the ground floor and were just wondering what to do next when Sammy and Mike came pelting toward us. We froze.

"Hey!" Sammy yelled. "You! Get out! Scatter! Cops everywhere. If they find those Help-for-Hire twerps in the basement we're all history!"

He and Mike bolted into the dining room and through to the kitchen just as the double doors that led to the parking lot burst open and a whole horde of uniformed police flooded in.

Greta Vortek was with them. And Officer Wildman. And Zim.

Zim saw us, came running over, threw his arms around Elmo, and then tried to hug all the rest of us at the same time.

"It worked!" Elmo gasped, almost smothered. "The car-tracking thing. It worked! It led you here."

"Like a charm," smiled Greta, coming up behind Zim. "And you leaving that trail of cookie crumbs by the curb was inspired, Nick. It gave Zim a good idea of what had happened. He called us right away. Mind you — we wouldn't have been certain that the theft of Zim's car and your kidnapping were linked if those idiots hadn't left their previous stolen car — the blue one — in Zim's parking spot!"

Tom gurgled with laughter.

"Can you believe our luck?" giggled Liz. "Of all the cars in Raven Hill to steal, Nick, your kidnappers picked Zim's."

"It was nice and new," I said. "They liked that. They've run out the side door, by the way."

"We'll get them," Greta said confidently. "Nowhere to hide out there. But it's The Wolf we really want. He escaped from jail, you know, just yesterday afternoon, while he was being trans-ferred to a hospital. He'd been complaining of chest pains."

"He'd probably heard that almost all these kids had been grabbed and the job was nearly over," said Zim grimly. "He just couldn't resist seeing them suffer in person. He's like that. A monster. Well, his revenge instinct has done him in this time."

Wildman came up to us then, looking worried. "He's gotten away," he said grimly. "There must have been a tip-off."

"Oh, no," I said calmly. "He's here. We trapped him in the basement. Below the machine room, just past the swimming pool. But you want to be very careful getting him out. I think he's armed."

It was a huge pleasure to see Wildman's jaw drop. He cleared his throat. "You . . . trapped him?" he asked after a moment.

"There are a few other people with him," Richelle said sweetly. "Well, two actually *with* him . . ."

"And six locked in a room right at the back," I finished for her. "You'll probably get a surprise when you see them. They look a lot like us."

Zim and Greta Vortek exchanged amazed glances. Wildman ran his fingers through his hair and hurried away.

They sent us home in the back of a police van just after that. They didn't want us to stay around, in case there was any violence, and the six of us couldn't fit in an ordinary car. We could have gone in two cars, but there was no way we'd agree to be separated.

Zim sat in the front seat with the driver. And it was Zim who told us, as the message came through, that there had been a showdown, and The Wolf was dead. Not because of a bullet, but because of a massive heart attack.

We were all incredibly relieved. It hadn't been so good to think that we had an enemy like The Wolf in the world. Prison didn't seem to make him any less dangerous.

"They got the kids out of the basement," Zim murmured. "Not much the worse for wear. They say they're your doubles, all right."

Richelle tossed her head. "The one who's supposed to look like me doesn't really look like me at *all*!" she exclaimed. "Her hair's bleached. I'm sure of it. And her eyes just aren't . . ."

"They *do* look a lot like us," Sunny said positively.

"Especially in a group," Elmo agreed. "It's fascinating. It must have taken months to find them. They must have been picked out of hundreds of people."

"Thousands," said Tom, rolling his eyes.

"It's so strange to think that there are people around who look like us, and who've been taught to act like us as well," said Liz dreamily. "Strange to think we all have doubles."

"Only to people who don't know us well," I said, looking around at them all. "I couldn't mistake anyone for any of you for more than a second. You're all unique."

"Are you being emotional or insulting, Kontellis?" grinned Tom.

"Work it out for yourself," I jeered. But I smiled to myself in the jolting darkness of that van as it sped along the highway that led to home.

One day we'll all be grown up. I thought. *Liz will be a writer. Elmo will be the editor of the* Pen. *Tom will be an artist – or a cartoonist. He'll enjoy that. Richelle will be in the fashion business for sure. Sunny will be the best gym coach ever, unless she ends up as a Navy SEAL or something. I'll be – what? – an executive in a big computer company, maybe.*

But whatever happens, and however old we get, in our hearts we'll be the same people as we are now, my thoughts ran on. *A weird sort of bunch. Incredibly different from one another. But friends. Good friends. For always.*

Thanks to Help-for-Hire Inc.

THE END

Thrilling tales of adventure and danger...

Emily Rodda's

DELTORA

Enter the realm of monsters, mayhem, and magic of Deltora Quest, Deltora Shadowlands, and Dragons of Deltora

Gordon Korman's

ON THE RUN

The chase is on in this heart-stopping series about two fugitive kids who must follow a trail of clues to prove their parents' innocence.

Gregor the Overlander
by Suzanne Collins

In the Underland, Gregor must face giant talking cockroaches, rideable bats, and a legendary Rat King to save his family, himself, and maybe the entire subterranean world.

Available wherever you buy books.